Alice Dwyer-Joyce was born in Birr in Ireland and educated privately and at Alexandra College, Dublin. She took her medical degree in the College of Surgeons and entered general practice, in partnership with her husband, in a Cambridgeshire village, where they have remained for over forty years. They have one son and two grandchildren.

Her writing began while she was learning German from an au pair student. The difficulty of finding the right word in a foreign language led her to write first in English, and since then she has produced over thirty novels. The interest she feels in people and the love she bears for the quiet and humour of village life both in England and in Ireland are clearly seen in her writing.

# GIBBET FEN

Lalage's grandfather, Dr Robert Lister, had been the last in a long line of Listers who had served the village as doctors, all of them loved and respected by their patients for their kindness and humanity. After his death, the whole village eagerly awaits the new doctor's arrival. But when Jonathan Cunningham takes up his post Lalage finds his manner upsetting, she resents his interference in her family's problems, and finds his immediate success with the villagers galling.

*Books by Alice Dwyer-Joyce*
*Published by The House of Ulverscroft:*

THE MOONLIT WAY
THE DIAMOND CAGE
THE GINGERBREAD HOUSE
THE BANSHEE TIDE
FOR I HAVE LIVED TODAY
THE STROLLING PLAYERS
PRESCRIPTION FOR MELISSA
DANNY BOY
THE GLITTER-DUST
DOCTOR ROSS OF HARTON
THE STORM OF WRATH
THE PENNY BOX
THE RAINBOW GLASS
CRY THE SOFT RAIN
THE SWIFTEST EAGLE
THE CHIEFTAIN

ALICE DWYER-JOYCE

---◆---

# GIBBET FEN

*Complete and Unabridged*

# ULVERSCROFT
*Leicester*

First published in Great Britain in 1984 by
Robert Hale Limited
London


First Large Print Edition
published 1999
by arrangement with
Robert Hale Limited
London

British Library CIP Data

Dwyer-Joyce, Alice
    Gibbet Fen.—Large print ed.—
    Ulverscroft large print series: romance
    1. Love stories
    2. Large type books
    I. Title
    823.9′14 [F]

ISBN 0–7089–4133–8

Published by
F. A. Thorpe (Publishing) Ltd.
Anstey, Leicestershire

Set by Words & Graphics Ltd.
Anstey, Leicestershire
Printed and bound in Great Britain by
T. J. International Ltd., Padstow, Cornwall

This book is printed on acid-free paper

'Where the hell are you taking me?' the farmer asked, as he lay in the fen mud. It had been quite a task to lever the tractor off his leg. The morphia I had given him was beginning to work.

'To Addenbrooke's Hospital, of course,' I replied. He squinted up at me.

'Do you know, were I to be writing a book, I'd dedicate it to that there place.'

So here it is:

To Addenbrooke's Hospital,
Cambridge.

# The Lone Tree

There is a Lone Tree in my life
That once was sap-green, tender and with
   bark
That scraped and wept.
But as it grew and was more rigid in the
   wind
The lichened years of grey and rowan-grey
Tried to fill the letters cut so deep to reach
   the core of me.
And now in winter's stormy greet
I trace my finger in the scar of years
And know I lived the magic age.

                         Robert Dwyer-Joyce

# 1

I stood at the foot of the open grave and raised my eyes to the sage-green corduroy velvet of the tiles on the church roof trying to will myself not to cry. If I started I would never be able to leave off. So far I had felt completely detached about what was happening. I had moved across the stage of a marionette theatre acting out a play that had no reality about it. Then the snowdrops had undone my false calm. They were ribboned in a paper frill laced and pretty and just now I had taken a step forward and thrown them down past the moss that lined the grave to lie on the top of the coffin. The thick oak with its burnished brass plate had in no way blotted out the shock of white hair and the tufted eyebrows . . . the serene handsome face. There was a pain in my chest such as no marionette had ever suffered. Yet the roof was no comfort to me for I remembered the day I had gone out on rounds with him in the car on just such a day and I not six years old dressed in my new velvet corduroy coat.

'Look at the saffron of the sun on the old roof up there, Lalage.'

1

He had smiled across at me and told me that he imagined God had given the church a new coat for Christmas too and I thought that could not be true for the tiles had been there hundreds of years. The same coloured mosses grew on many of the old fen cottage roofs but then he would know that. To my mind he knew everything.

'There's music in your name, Lalage,' he went on. 'Annie told me you don't like it because the village people get it wrong but it's a wonderful name and you'll learn about it when you go to school . . . La . . . la . . . gee. Lalage of the laughing smile. When you go to school in Southwold you'll have to tackle Horace and his Odes . . . and all the rest of it.

'And I've lost Britain, I've lost Gaul . . . and I've lost Rome and worst of all I've lost Lalage.'

For a moment I could almost hear the echo of his voice in the churchyard but I knew it was impossible.

I watched the way the wind billowed the Vicar's surplice and lifted the hair on his brow. It whipped the richness from his voice too and I wondered if he were wishing for the service to be over so that he could get to the fire in Church House where the surgery was and where we lived. He had no intention of hurrying over the burial of his old friend for his words were slow and measured.

'I heard a voice from Heaven saying unto me Write, From henceforth blessed are the dead which die in the Lord: even so saith the Spirit for they rest from their labours . . .'

I concentrated on the great block of granite beside him as if I had never seen it before though I knew it by heart.

It was the epitaph of the first Robert Lister . . . the epitaph of them all.

HERE LIES THE BODY OF ROBERT LISTER PHYSICIAN AND SURGEON OF THE PARISH FOR FIFTY THREE YEARS WHO DIED ON THE TWENTY FIRST OF MAY IN THE YEAR EIGHTEEN HUNDRED AND EIGHTY EIGHT.

MOST RARE IN THIS WORLD HE WAS A MAN WITH NO THOUGHTS OF SELF AN APOTHECARY WITH NEITHER POMP NOR PRIDE.

HIS HAND WAS OPEN IN LIFE AND EVER GENEROUS. IN DEATH HE SHALL NEVER BE FORGOTTEN. HIS CHARITY IN HIS PROFESSION ENTITLES HIM TO BE CALLED THE BELOVED PHYSICIAN OF THE POOR.

3

LET OTHER INSCRIPTIONS BOAST HONOURS AND PEDIGREE AND RICHES. HERE LIES A MAN WHO LOVED HIS FELLOW MEN.

His son had been my great great grandfather and he had had a son Robert and a grandson Robert. Always that was how it had been in St Agnes Parva but there was an end to it now ... an end to the tradition of the Beloved Physician of the Poor. My eye went down the inscriptions to Surg. Lieut. Robert William Lister who had been lost at sea in the Second World War and who had been my father. They had polished another side of the block to add his name and later the name of my mother who had given her life for her country too. My mother had put me in charge of Annie and Grandfather and had joined the W.R.N.S. and then there had been a blitz on Plymouth and all chance of begatting another Robert Lister had gone ...

They were saying the Lord's Prayer and I knew we should soon be back to the house. I glanced at Annie and I saw that she had not surrendered to the luxury of tears. Her face was white and set. Her hands in her cotton gloves were tight-gripped together. Louisa her daughter looked ill. We should never have let Louisa come to the grave. Grandfather would never have allowed it. He had been worried about her. She was to have a baby and he had told me that she was far past the age for it. It was a miracle of conception he had confided to me but maybe the good Lord knew what He was about. Grandfather had known he was dying and he had told me that they were all my responsibility once he was gone. My shoulders were strong enough he said for all that I was 'his wee mouse.'

There were a great throng of people in the churchyard and they stood aside to let us pass by . . . important prosperous folk but humbler folk too, the ones the first Robert Lister had loved best. Louisa went to Sam's wheel-chair and Sam's bright face was downcast. Sam had been boatswain on my father's ship and Sam had escaped with his life but afterwards he had got ill and eventually had been invalided out of the Navy and had come home to live with us, for he was Louisa's husband. It seemed that we were to have one disaster after another for he had been diagnosed as disseminated sclerosis so now Louisa was fussing about the wheel-chair and trying to push it along the gravelled path.

'I'll see to it, Louisa.'

That had been Grandfather's answer to grief . . . to find somebody worse than yourself, but Louisa did not want help.

5

'There'll be important people wanting to speak to you,' she told me but I held on to the chair as she tucked the rug more securely round Sam and we went together with one hand on Sam's shoulder and the other on the handle of the chair.

'Nobody as important as Sam,' I said. 'He's the man of the house now.'

They had made Brown's field into a car-park as they always did for big funerals and the police were trying to keep the traffic in order. The engines were starting and the cars bounced over the tufty grass. There were so many people to be talked to and thanked . . . representatives from so many different Institutions and the Salvation Army Band and the British Legion and the Health Authority . . . the Methodist Parson and the Baptist Minister. The Women's Institute, the Cricket Club, members of the Country Council, First Aid, Fire Service . . . crowds of people who had come and last of all when I was almost in a panic, almost ready to run home where many of the people would presently come to meet in the big sitting-room and drink sherry . . . last of all I saw the strangest mourner of them all. I caught a glimpse of him in the rookery high in the bare branches of the winter trees. It was the gypsy boy from Gibbet Fen. He was like a magpie and he was given to bright colours. He had collected a rag of scarlet cloth and it gave him away for he had found a hollow in a big chestnut tree high above the church and had made himself a hide. The Salvation Army Brass Band would have drawn him and maybe he had not been able to resist it. The Band was on its way off now but stepping slow.

*The Lord's my Shepherd, I'll not want,*
*He makes me down to lie*
*In pastures green, He leadeth me*
*The quiet waters by.*
*He leadeth me, He leadeth me*
*The quiet waters by...*

They were out in the High Street now and marching away down the village and the music was fading and still I was confused with the throng of the congregation. Inspector Bullen gave me a smart salute as I passed by but my thoughts had stuck in the hide high in the chestnut-tree with 'Squirrel Nutkin'. It was I who had given him the name and that was what we called him in Church House. He was a strange creature and nobody could tell you his age but he wandered all about the countryside and mostly he lived rough. He belonged to the clan of Smiths who were encamped on Gibbet Fen, a lonely part of black fen three miles from the edge of Agnes Parva with a black pool that had a sinister air to it . . . and a clump of miserable poplars and a deal of rubbish and old tin cans. The children teased him when he came into the village but they had no ill-will for him. Their mothers would feed him on the doorstep at the back of the cottages. He had a jackdaw that perched on his shoulder and the jackdaw spoke but he did not — never had. His left leg dragged behind him. His neck was awry and questioning and he was as nimble as a cricket. So I had called him 'Squirrel Nutkin' from years ago. I thought the name suited his strange wildness and his eagerness in the quest for knowledge.

I stood outside the gates of the church and remembered Squirrel Nutkin and old Mr Brown and how the squirrels had sailed across to the island with their tails high to catch the wind in a flotilla every year.

'Old Mr Brown, will you favour us with permission to gather nuts up on your island?' Squirrel Nutkin had been the impertinent one full of riddles.

'The man in the wilderness said to me,
'How many strawberries grow in the sea?'
I answered him as I thought good —

8

'As many red herrings as grow in the wood."

Grandfather had called him little St Francis of Assisi for he said he had this thing with wild animals and birds. He was known for it. They brought dying creatures to him and he lived in a wooden shack near the gypsy encampment. His hands had the art of healing so Grandfather had said.

He was leaving the hide now yet it was almost impossible to see him go and I was surrounded by a great many people. One moment he was there with just that flash of scarlet and then he was gone like a squirrel indeed, flying down the trunk of the ancient chestnut and then like a flash up to yet a higher branch and away. I wakened myself out of a fugue and I was late in the sitting-room. Louisa and Sam were gone and many of the congregation. The Salvation Army was a dying strain down at the corner by the Conservative Club. I hurried across the road to the Regency mansion . . . no pretension of grandeur there but it had been ours for so long and now it was mine. I saw how it was staffed by Annie who had lived there for sixty years . . . and Annie's daughter, Louisa Fraser, S.R.N . . . Sam in the wheel-chair.

Louisa was due to have Sam's baby in ten

weeks . . . 'Bosun Sam.'

Then I was in the centre of the sitting-room and the log fire was a glory.

I heard the hum of voices and could think of nothing. 'So sad for it to happen at Christmas . . . makes it so much worse. Dr Bob gave his life to the village and his son your dad gone in the war . . . and your mum too. Ain't it a pity that you weren't medical? You could have taken their places. Don't know how we'll do without a Dr Lister at Church House.'

Annie had taken off her coat and put on a white apron and was in charge of the sherry tray. Louisa was circulating with some petit fours and little triangular sandwiches. I found James John Bryan leaning against the corner of the mantelpiece and he looked at me with concern. He had three glasses of sherry stored behind the clock and he passed one to me and told me to drink it down. Then he took one to keep me company and when we had finished them I found another full glass in my hand.

'Blast all these ghouls,' he said. 'Why the hell can't they have the decency to go to their own homes? God! The value the people put on the panoply of death . . . like vultures at a feast.'

I had had two glasses of sherry and another full in my hand now and the faces were swimming around me like goldfish in a bowl and I had a pain in my chest and I could hear a jackdaw somewhere. I knew there were no jackdaws . . . only a memory . . . an echo of Squirrel Nutkin in the hide at the top of the chestnut tree.

'The man in the wilderness said to me,

'How many strawberries grow in the sea . . .' ' I thought.

James John Bryan took the third glass of sherry out of my hand and set it back on the mantelpiece.

'Take it easy, Lalage. You've had a terrible time and you must take a holiday and get away from it all. Go somewhere and find some young people like yourself. You've had no youth except boarding school shut up here in this little village. Choir practice and Women's Institute . . . and coffee mornings and sick-visiting.'

'Jaaack!'

The jackdaw was somewhere about and I asked James John if he heard it too.

'Quoth the raven 'Nevermore!" he said. 'Why the hell did you not marry me when I asked you?'

'You're perfectly happy as you are,' I said and then Dr Camps of Agnes Magna appeared between us and took my hand in his.

'I must get along, Lalage. Look after yourself and ring me if there's any problem in the practice. Luckily things are not busy at the moment. I'm glad to be of help.'

'We'll get by.'

Any thanks were inadequate. He was covering our area till the Council had time to elect the new man for Agnes Parva. Then in a moment he had gone and the Clerk of the Executive Council was there, his face studied in its solemnity. I tried to pay attention to what he was saying and all the time my mind wandered but at last he was bidding me farewell and they were all moving towards the door and away. Mr Hall the Clerk was very sad. He thanked me for the use of the old surgery pro tem.

'I noticed that the surgery step is hollowed out by patients' feet. The first brass plate was never changed and why should it have been? It was the same name. ROBERT LISTER. Maybe a blind man could feel it still written there.'

They were gone at last, all but James John and he started to act like a solicitor now but he put another glass of sherry into my hands and told me I needed a refill though I doubted it. We'd best discuss the future. 'My father has talked about the will at length . . . '

His father was James Bryan. The firm was James Bryan and Son and the son was James John Bryan. Agnes Parva never called the son anything but Mr James John. It was all in the order of things in old villages . . .

James John was advising me to sell out to the incoming doctor and somehow he and I were sitting down to lunch in the dining-room.

We were eating cold game pie made by Annie and a salad. James John had a tankard of beer and I had no need of more alcohol. Black coffee was brewing in the Cona beside me.

'So you see there was practically no capital. Shares are not what they used to be. You should sell out to the new doctor. The chap will have to have the house and surgery and we could put the price up a bit. There's no other big house to match this one and the people are used to it. You could build a bungalow and invest the balance wisely though I doubt if you'd live on the interest.'

'I could get a job,' I said. 'I have the others to think of.'

'What others?' he demanded, and I told him Annie and the Frazers . . . all one big family. He asked me if I were daft.

'A bungalow would be just the thing for

Sam then,' he said. 'Sam crippled with disseminated sclerosis. But if you insist on being pig-headed about it I know it was your Grandfather's idea. There would be Sam's pension and Nurse Frazer could take a nursing post and Annie might find a domestic post but she's rather old for a change now.'

'They will all stay on here.'

Annie had come in to clear away and I saw that her ramrod back had lost its stiffness and she gave a little sigh. She was put out with James John and told him to stop upsetting me and she cleared off smartly forgetting to take the table cloth, and came back for it in time to hear me say again that we were one family and we would sink or swim together. Then she was gone and I wondered how I could be only twenty-one years of age when I felt as old as Methuselah.

'Have you thought of the rates and taxes?' James John demanded . . . and I told him it was one of my favourite worries so we might as well sink and be done with it.

Annie had gone off to the kitchen to fetch the sweet and James John leaned towards me and spoke in a secret voice.

'Sell out for the highest price we can get. Go up to London and buy yourself a wardrobe of new clothes. Get value out of life before it's too late to enjoy it. Find yourself a

14

husband and settle down. Who are you going to meet in this dead-and-alive hole? I know you've always lived here but you've been tangled up in good works. It's a tender prison. Have fun for a change.'

For a moment I saw myself through his eyes . . . a poor little girl with my out-of-date hair up in a beehive on top of my head . . . village institute on Thursday, choir practice on Friday . . . president of the ladies' sewing guild. I rarely went to the cinema and never to a dance. I read good books and between sleeping and waking I dreamt dreams that one day a prince would come in shining armour. He was very real this chap in armour on a white charger and always he waited about the corners of my mind. He would lift me up to sit on the saddle before him, and take me to a castle with turrets and marble floors. His face was like the knight in the stained-glass window in church near our pew kneeling to his sword at vigil.

'Have you ever been kissed, properly kissed?' my solicitor demanded and I felt the colour that flooded my cheeks. Almost I reminded him that my last living relative had just died and he should think shame of himself for talking to me in such a way. I was glad to see Annie come in with the trifle and hold it ready for me to help myself and her

15

mind was on her defence of me.

'There will be no need of wages for me and mine,' she said and looked at James John as if he was still five years of age and had called for me to go to Sunday school. 'I've never known any other home than this and I brought Miss Lalage up from the day she was born. Her mother gave her into my hands at the finish when it was all destroyed on us and she's been like my own child. I have a bit of money put by and Sam has his sick pay and his pension from the Navy. Louisa is a trained S.R.N. She's beholden to nobody and after the baby is born she can get herself a good job. We won't see the house sold out to strangers who will turn it into matchbox flats and paint it all the colours of the rainbow. This is where Miss Lalage was born Sir and this is where she'll abide. We might have to rent off the surgery premises to the new doctor but that would be fittin'. The patients have found themselves coming to this same waiting room since eighteen thirty-five and that was before my time I can tell you.'

James was helping himself to the trifle and telling Annie that nobody could make sherry trifle like herself, but she had wandered into my history which he knew as well as she did. I had been set to read medicine and I had been taken with the spot on my lung.

16

'That was the end of medicine for her. She ended up in Papworth poor dear and she got well but not well enough.'

I wished she would stop telling him what he knew but her hand on my hair was very kind and I loved her dearly.

Still I was glad when we were interrupted as Louisa Frazer came in to tell us that we had a patient to be seen. I excused myself and went back with Louisa to find Michael Pegg and his mother in the surgery. His eyes were fixed hopefully on the old sweet jar and he told me he didn't want no needle. He had it last year so he was paid up for 'lock-jaw'. Between us we settled for a dressing and of course some sweets. It was not a case that would call Dr Camps from Magna.

'Sharpe's Super Cream Toffees' I told Michael . . . fresh in from Mrs Marshall this week. 'I like the mint ones best and you can help yourself to six. Any ones you like but to my mind the mint ones are best . . . green they're . . .'

God help me I knew I had had a vocation. This sort of thing was not hard labour. Life would have been a joy and full of happiness. At the moment Michael Pegg was showing me what might have been. He had picked out six green toffees and had given me one and maybe he had broken my heart but the next moment he had filled me with laughter.

'Glad I had done with the old prick. It would have been bad enough if you pricked me but they say we're to have a foreign bugger in Agnes . . . '

'They'll elect a new doctor in the Executive Council,' I told Michael, 'he'll be the best there is. They will choose him and he'll come as soon as he can. You'll get along fine together.'

'Don't want anybody else but Old Doctor Bob,' he said. 'He brung me into the world and he cared for me. Time a pigeon I had flew against the wire and cut its crop open and he got a needle and stitched up that pigeon as good as new . . . let the whole surgery wait whiles he done it . . . said it never cried and that was to be an example to me.'

'He'll be the best man there is,' I said, 'the new man.'

So a medical student's life was not for me and I knew it. By the time I got back to the dining-room the solicitor was gone and I was glad.

My gramp's words were in my ears.

'By God Lalage it's time we smashed the cure of *disseminated sclerosis*. We've worked at it for years. Here we are and Sam will never walk again. Poor Bo'sun! He'll never

18

lose his cheerfulness till the day he dies
. . . but die he will. He'll never get better for
all the dust we've thrown into Louisa's eyes
but she knows it. The good Lord saw fit to
send them a child.' Gramp's been very low
that day. 'You'll have to see to it Lalage. I
appoint you as my locum tenens.' These were
almost the old man's last words and they put
a weight on my heart. 'You'll have to see to it,
Lalage of the sweet laughter. *Dulce ridentem
Lalagen amabo* I will love you.'

That was how he had died and the fact of it
burnt into my soul. 'They served my family
all my life little mouse . . . It's a sad thing to
have a brand new plate in St Agnes Parva but
that's the way it goes. You'll see to it for me.'

So I was now the owner of an immense
Regency mansion . . . with no pretence of
luxury. I had lost my father in the battle of
the Western Approaches . . . my mother soon
after in an air raid on Plymouth . . . a Queen
Wren. Here I was with the solicitor taken
himself off and Sam coming searching for
me.

'So they're all gone, Lalage, reckon it's time
for you and me to creosote the barn.'

We had discussed the future but we had
come to no definite arrangement. It seemed
likely that the incoming doctor would build
himself a new bungalow. They were going up

like small mushrooms in Agnes Parva. I stood on top of a steep cliff when I thought of moving out of my house. It had been difficult not to have looked in James John's face and begged him not to see me turned out but he had left after the lunch when I had been seeing to the surgery and Sam was there now. James John had read the last will and testament . . . the whole place was mine to administer but there was practically no capital . . . Annie was hovering about me now saying that I must eat or I would die. In the surgery I had dismissed what might be the last satisfied customer of the Listers.

Sam waited for me in the dining room and I knew that his thoughts and mine ran side by side. 'This decent black of mine, Bo'sun, it's in no way fitten to use it if we're going to creosote the barn. I'll change into slacks and sweater for that but one thing I have to do. They'll all be gone away now and I want to say goodnight to Gramp. Then this evening or tomorrow or the next day you and I will paint the barn . . . time it was done. The worst of the winter is still to come.'

He looked at me from the wheel-chair and I recalled all the times he had fallen over on his face and come up smiling, the wide desperate enamelled smile. It was a joke between us that if either of us was in despair we painted the barn. We had done it the day the specialist had told me I had T.B . . . We had done it the day James John had announced his engagement to Lucy Miller and I had only myself to thank for that. He knew I must look after Gramp and Church House. Then I had left off creosoting the barn till after the wedding. I realised that Lucy was a pretty girl and that she was bright and gay. I had brushed the pain out on the black wood walls of the big old barn and I had thought that Sam had a sorrow to brush away too. He had been finished with his days as a naval petty officer in the Western Approaches a long time. His sight had given him a warning. His skipper my father was dead and gone. He had come out of hospital with a deadly diagnosis, all wrapped up in four words . . . *multiple sclerosis . . . multiple sclerosis . . .* invalided out.

'Come across to the grave, Sam,' I said. 'Let's say goodnight to master God rest him.'

We idled round the grave and looked at the cards on the wreaths and I read them out to Sam. It was maybe the last wreath I recognised as coming from the Smith clan of gypsies. It was a log of holly and another to cross it and decorated with the everlasting flowers that the tinkers always brought to the back door . . . the Smiths of the Gibbet Fen.

'He was up there in the chestnut tree. Did you see him?' Sam asked me and I nodded my head.

'Squirrel Nutkin that was what you called him.' Sam smiled. 'He came down smartish at the finish and went off with the Band but he was back again later. I heard the little old jackdaw but St Francis made himself scarce. The police would have run him off but he was too smart for them he had the jackdaw hid in his pocket.'

I wanted to talk to somebody and I picked on Sam or maybe Sam picked on me. He said we must plan for the creosoting of the barn. It was too dark now. There was time to fetch the creosote from the village stores now and if we pushed the chair up the street we could fetch the creosote and start on the job first thing in the morning. It was turning very cold and the wind was due east. We got to the stores with Sam turning the wheels and me pushing. The transaction was soon done and Len Marshall was kind enough to offer to run us home in his van. I was so used to seeing the way Sam made light of what was the failing power in his lower limbs. He hauled himself up by two powerful arms and lifted his legs up to follow him first one and then the other never losing the cheerfulness. Back at Church House we found ourselves at the barn and it took Len a moment or two to open the door and get the chair down ready. Then Len lifted him as gently, as easily as if he were lifting a child and set him in his world again. The barn was called 'the workhouse' by the family but Sam and I had glorified it soon after Sam took over. I had always thought of it as 'Treasure Island'. There had been the time when I had read the book to Sam when he was bed-bound. It had been a project between us to re-christen the workhouse. It was now the *Admiral Benbow Inn*. Together we had painted a discarded sign that I had begged from the Duke of Wellington pub in the High Street and it was a wonderful thing. It made the Bo'sun better, I was convinced it did. Gramps always agreed. There was a charisma about that sign that I will never forget. It would draw me home from the other side of the world. The Duke of Wellington had been transformed into the Admiral Benbow and his cocked hat. He even swung in the wind and creaked. You could hear the noise in the night eerily like a Hong Kong prayer bell even from the house faintly. Annie called it a 'dratted noise', said there was a haunt in it. She told me that if I didn't stop my nonsense I'd have Blind Pugh tap-tap-tapping his stick up the avenue to knock with his gnarled fist on our kitchen door.

All the same the barn was a super place. It had served generations of the Listers and it had gathered memories. There was a secluded corner of the big barn and it was furnished with things that had been used and loved and discarded. There were two wheel-backed chairs and an old kitchen table. Then for work there was a grindstone, a lathe and a saw-bench, a mitre-frame, a box of nails, a kitchen cupboard that had mugs and cups on hooks and plates and drawers with anything you might want. From somewhere long ago came the Toby jugs ranged over the old fire. The Adam grate was beautiful and useful too and had a chimney. We had fuel to collect in the fens, bits of ash trees or willows. We 'borrowed' lumps of coal from the house.

Len Marshall had often visited us before and now he put a match to the fire and gave his opinion as he always did.

'Cor!' he exclaimed, 'this place is a treat . . . don't know nothing like it. Times I come in the door and light the fire as I done now and see the Bo'sun reach down the sherry and the Bovril. I'm back in the Western Approaches and the deck rising under my feet. Brave men . . . brave ships.'

Len had served on Father's ship and if they got back to the war days I'd never get rid

24

of him. I helped Sam fix the sherry in the mugs . . . the Bovril, and waited for the water to boil. Soon we were all sitting in front of the singing kettle and Sam out of the old steel chair to the comfort of a chair that had belonged to my Grandmother a long time past. When we had finished the ginger snaps which were stale and we liked them like that Len produced four horse brasses which he had brought to cheer us up.

'There's some work for you, Miss Lalage.'

There was the business of deciding a place to set them and we took our time about this matter for it was of great importance and I had to find the Brasso. Two of the brasses went one side and two the other of the Adam grate at each side of the *Victory*. They were perfect. The fire was brighter than before as it reflected the brass. Maybe I could stay here for ever and never face the cruel world that waited outside Church House. There was a tortoise stove that kept the barn warm always and burnt up slack and rubbish and garnered wood we got from the fens. It was Annie's brain child for she was never done whittling about my weak chest though that was all in the past now. It had departed and faded to a yearly visit to the Clinic. My chair in the Admiral Benbow Inn was the blue Windsor with the ears so that the draughts might not blow on me! I had the best view from there of the model of the *Victory* that the Bo'sun had made. I smiled as I looked up at the special shelf, the ship full rigged and with all the canvas set dressed overall. I did not know the half of it but I never forget the tragedy. It had been a wonderful work of art and it had been finished, just a point of soldering to do. Then Sam had forgotten the blow torch for maybe ten seconds. He had sent a salvo roaring across the rigging and the careful cordage was gone. It had all been replaced over months of fiddling work . . . and that smile had never gone out. Len was looking at the craft now and he sighed.

'That was well done,' he said. 'I'd have burnt the bugger in the stove . . . I swear I would if it was me.'

He went off after a while reluctant to go but there were the orders to get out in the shop and the Missus wouldn't thank him if he left the job to her. We said goodbye and thanked him for lifting us home. Then we settled ourselves by the grate. There was something Sam wanted to ask me. I knew him of old and as usual he took his time. Then he got it out. It seemed that Louisa had spoken to him about me and he wanted to ask if I was 'whittling' about something.

26

There was that word again.

Louisa had overheard Mr James John talking to me.

'There was nothing strange about that,' I muttered. 'He had his work to do.'

'Louisa heard him ask you to-day why you hadn't married *him*,' he said. 'It was a nice thing to say and him married to Miss Lucy.'

'Louisa says more than her prayers,' I said. 'I admit it did surprise me a bit . . . maybe worried me a bit too. I know well that she was right for him and if he had rebounded from me to her it was the way it was. She was pretty and bright and gay. I had refused him and maybe hurt him. I had Gramp to think of and the whole set-up here. I couldn't run off and leave you all. Besides he did better for himself. Do you remember how we painted this barn then, Bo'sun?'

'It seems the way we work out our sorrows, Miss, but he's still in love with you. You should have taken him, now you'd have your own house and a man to look after you. You're tied to Church House now like Andromeda was chained to a rock. You're a lovely young girl and Mrs James John can't hold a candle to you for all her fine feathers. There are boys in the district that hang round the church door Sundays in the chance you'll take notice of them. You've got a great capacity for loving mankind and you'd make a fine wife. You've taken after your Mother and she was a kind of harbour a sailor might find after a long storm at sea . . . and find rest and tranquillity instead of destruction in a Plymouth blitz.'

He was very sad so I grinned at him and told him to pass me a file from the bench. 'O.K. then, Sam, pass me the file. I'll saw my chain off and sling my hook.'

'I warn you my lass there's such a storm coming up the sky that you'll be sorry for yourself. Sling your hook indeed! You're getting to speak like a common deckhand.' I smiled at him and reminded him that tomorrow we must finish the creosoting of the Admiral Benbow Inn.

'Then we'll batten down the hatches and sail away into the future and God bless us and all who sail with us.'

# 2

Things did not improve very visibly in the days that followed. For one thing we began to get the prospective candidates for the post as doctor and as there was a possibility that we might sell the house or at any rate rent off the surgery part they all came and most of them plus wives . . . to view the house. We got used to the squeak of brakes in the drive and the covert screwing down of the car windows for the first appraisal of the premises. They were professional gentlemen. They did not say openly what they thought of this great rambling place, but it was readable in their faces. They wanted to bring down the price. They criticised it politely and the anger grew in me because I loved it.

There was no central heating. It wanted decorating from top to bottom. The kitchen was an early Victorian museum piece. The garden was far too big. It would take two men to keep it properly but that might be to the good. It could be sold off for building a housing estate . . . bring in some cash . . . the wives were agreed that the kitchen was archaic and they did not like all the great oak

29

beams and the polished copper pans. There wasn't the time for this sort of stuff. The surgery accommodation was out of Charles Dickens. The floor must come up and the whole area be tiled and that cost money these days. The end wall must be knocked out to give light. The filing cabinets wanted reorganising from A to Z. You could buy metal units these days. The receptionist saw to all that. Where did she sit? She must be able to keep the patients separated from the doctor. If we had a good receptionist she would do most of the work. Where had we sited the lavatories? You had to be careful about that. They had noticed that Agnes Parva had no 'public loos'. If the 'doc' wasn't wily the natives would take over the conveniences.

Then there was another thing. They all assumed that we shared the practice with the man from Agnes Magna . . . weekend about.

'Dr Camps . . . Dr Camps . . . Dr Camps. Agnes Magna,' I stuttered. 'He's covering us now. He likes to do his own cases but in an emergency he's always there, 'knock for knock' they call it.'

'How quaint,' the young wife said. The wives were the worst. They were all very sophisticated and many of them thought I was an adolescent . . . did not know how I

loved the fen and the lovely timelessness of it
. . . the slow passage of the days and the
warmth of people's hearts . . . the good
neighbour policy when it was a normal thing
to 'run in to the poor old dear next door and
bring a bate of stew and dumplings and the
first of the new potatoes and peas' . . . and it
might be Feast Sunday . . . I thought that
these things lasted for ever . . . were kind of
eternal . . . and now the combine harvester
had come and upset us and the straw was
burnt. It should never have been burnt. The
cattle ate it, the horses bedded down in it up
to their shining chests. It was the stuff that
was the life of the fen and they were burning
it . . .

I knew we lived twenty miles from the
nearest 'good shops' but nobody was better
than Len Marshall. There was no decent
hairdresser for miles. Did I not realise that
doctors organised their own lives. A doctor's
life was not 'all work and no play' any longer.
It was time I got out and lived. Had I got a
regular boy friend?

I made no hit with any of them. I knew it. I
fought for the trees in the orchard. These
trees had been all matched by Laxton's, an
old firm in Bedford, and they were pruned to
bear fruit. They must not give way to a
housing estate. Old Pegg of garden path saw

31

to the pruning of them and the spraying against the moth and they had borne fruit every year, enough to supply almost the whole little village. They must not be hauled up like rotten teeth and killed. It was murder!

'But I'd want to lay down a tennis court there,' said one wife.

'Well you can't,' I choked. 'It's not for sale. It will never be for sale, never, never, never . . . never.'

'That's not what the Clerk of the Council said. He hinted that you weren't all that well off. He said we must wait and see but not expect you to sell your fortress lightly.'

Sam and I were creosoting the barn steadily and maybe it kept me sane. It went on for weeks and always came these invaders but I was the one that was out of step, not them. They were all young people struggling up the flow of life like elvers, spawned eels striving to live against the flow of the fall. I knew it. Mine was the fault and I was fighting an impossible battle for survival.

We got very slowly on with the Admiral Benbow Inn. The day before the last candidate was due weeks later I was finishing the last corner of a thirty-foot wall. By that time my jeans were past praying for. They had been dark green but Annie had boiled them to apple shade albeit patchy in parts. My sweater was green too, black-spotted from too much zeal with the creosote brush. My hair was in two thick plaits . . . one on each shoulder. A green bow beneath each ear . . . dark grass green and it matched my eyes and reflected green . . . dark dark dark. My tennis shoes were gaping at the toes and that gave me an Achilles heel and that was a laugh, but laughter had gone away . . . almost, I was weary and dispirited and Louisa was impatient with me and told me it was time I took my finger out. Louisa was irritable with her pregnancy and was taking it out on Sam and me, and Sam was miserable.

'It's all my fault,' he had confided in me. 'She was kind enough to marry me when I had drifted on a lee shore. She knew what she had married and I was selfish enough to let her do it . . . and it's my fault she's to have a baby. There's nothing I have to offer her. I'll never do a hand's turn again. There isn't any way it can work but I let her get pregnant and I probably killed her. She's not a young woman . . .'

'There were two of you in the bed Sam and a great love. It's fittin' Bo'sun. God maybe knew what He was doing.'

'But she's nigh enough forty-five to fifty years of age. It wasn't meant to be.'

I told him it *was* meant to be and he was to

33

shut his face. Louisa was a masterful woman like all sisters. She knew what she was doing like God and the baby would bring us all back to happiness. 'But I'll never be any better. I saw ex-naval blokes in the hospital worse nor me. It's a creeping thing, a thing that will destroy me till it takes my arms as well as my legs. I'll just lie helpless and I can't face it . . . not got the bottle to face the end of it.' I was on the ground at the foot of the ladder with a fresh can of creosote in my hand and I turned to confront him and knew it was time to say something but I had no idea what. I set the can down and I told Sam it was likely I would never talk to him again.

'Bugger me, Bo'sun. It was that bitch that said she'd pull up all the fruit trees and she destroyed you. I noticed she had the same effect on me and I'll blast her to hell if she hurt you as much as she hurt me. Sam! Sam! Sam! Maybe you'd have sacrificed your life for us as they did, the ones who didn't come home. Can't you see that you maybe gave Louisa the gift of a son? She could never have expected it and it's not just a baby. It's a *special* baby. It will be in your arms first of all. Then it will go crawling round the floor and be a damned nuisance. It will mix the flour in the salt and be smelly and dirty if we don't watch it. It will cry in the early hours of

34

the morning and smell like a civet cat of ammonia . . . if a civet cat smells of ammonia. I don't know. I only know it will be part of you, Bo'sun, and it means you'll have eternal life. You'll never die Sam . . . not now. You'll live on and it's not every man leaves a fine son behind him or even a girl.'

I was appalled to see the tears run down his face and all he said was 'I didn't see it like that. Eternal life! It's like that safe harbour. I thank you, Lalage of the *laughing* smile. The old master was never done talking about it. *Amabo* means 'I will love,' don't it? It's just right for you Miss, don't know one person that don't love you.'

He took himself off to see to the lawn mower but it was only to get out of my sight and he had a faith that gave him an excuse that we might ever want a sharp mower again. I settled myself back on the ladder weary and dispirited and afraid that I had said all the wrong things yet I could hear his voice in a distant part of the Admiral Benbow singing 'Land of Hope and Glory' and I thought of the *Victory* that had had its cordage blasted away in the blow-lamp blitz.

By now I was balanced on top of the ladder. The gravel scrunched in the drive behind me and over my shoulder I glimpsed a white sports car . . . long, low, stream-lined, obviously very expensive. It had a girl at the wheel and she was the most lovely creature I had ever seen. There was a sheen to her . . . a glamour. They did not see me at first for I was on the other angle of the house and that was what they had come to view or so I surmised. The girl got out of the car and discarded her head-scarf, carelessly opened back the front of her white fur coat. Her hair was white blonde too and went well with the coat. She was exquisite as she reached her arms towards the sky and gave a tinkling little laugh.

'You didn't tell me we were coming to Buck House!' she said and I saw the man get out from the seat and come to stand at her side. He was very dark and tall with a lank rangy kind of figure and his teeth were very white against the tan of his face as he smiled at her. He had a dark withdrawn expression and he said nothing but stood there looking up at the eaves of the house and she was petulant suddenly.

'Do we knock or ring or what duckie? There don't seem to be any of the native population about. I expect they've all 'up and hanged themselves'. Have you ever read 'Grantchester' by Rupert Brooke?' He turned round very slowly, pivoting on his heels and I knew he could not avoid seeing me now. I wished I could sneak off to the house and tidy up but there was no chance of that. He gave me a startled look and it was no wonder. I must have presented a strange spectacle for he said 'Good God!' and at that moment the ladder began to waver. He sprang across to try to save me from disaster. I remember thinking that if he were one of the prospective doctors at least he would be good in an emergency for he came across the intervening space in one bound but he was too late to save me. I sprawled at his feet and wished the earth had opened to engulf me. He put down a hand to my shoulder and asked me in concern if I were hurt. I sat there on the earth at his feet and grinned up at him.

'I usually come down like that. It's quicker.'

His face was still full of concern for me and I smelt the old familiar tang of doctor from him even above the creosote essence. I was sad all at once for it recalled the person I had loved best. His arm was round me and he was helping me to my feet and I stood there rubbing my backside ruefully with as much sophistication as a tom kitten. The girl sauntered over with an amused look on her face.

'Is your mummy anywhere about Poppet?' she asked me. 'We've come to look at the house and we're in rather a tearing rush as we have to get back to Wentbridge before nightfall.'

I brushed my plaits back from my shoulders but they promptly fell into their original position and I knew I looked like a grubby schoolgirl and had no rancour against her for thinking that was what I was. My voice was unrecognisable as my own when I managed to answer her and I could catch the spicy cut-pencil scent of her and envied her from the bottom of my heart. I wiped my hand down the side of my jeans inelegantly and held it out to her.

'I'm Lalage Lister. The house is mine and I'll show you over it. We've been creosoting the barn and I must apologise that I'm not fit to be seen.'

She looked down at my hand and raised an eyebrow and then I saw that it was all stained and not in any way a hand a person might wish to shake so I withdrew it and held it behind my back where presently the other hand joined it as we walked towards the house. I took them in by the front door for quite suddenly I wanted them to like my fortress.

The hall flags were scrubbed white and I was proud of them but the dining-room looked gloomy and the drawing-room was downright shabby, even if it was comfortable and homely.

I ran along to the kitchen to scrub my hands and to ask Annie to make us some tea and when I got back they were laughing together by the fireplace and I knew they were laughing at me because of their faces and the way they stopped up short when I came in.

'It's a teeny-weeny bit dank, don't you think?' the girl said and she laughed again and said they had forgotten their manners and had not introduced themselves. Her companion was Dr Jonathan Cunningham and she was Fenella, his fiancée.

'I have decided to eschew the gay life and give myself over to serving mankind . . . and what better way than becoming the wife of an earnest young doctor?'

He asked me rather abruptly if he could see the surgery premises and I walked before them down the passage and knew that later on in the lovely white car they would make great fun of the big bottle-green patch that Annie had insisted on putting into the seat of my jeans because they 'weren't decent'. I was ashamed of the surgery for the first time in my life. Up till now I had thought it a splendid exciting place but in a flash I saw it through their eyes for what it was . . . a great outmoded barn of a room with no facility for doing anything. Then in another second I was ashamed of myself too and felt I had betrayed Grandfather. Dr Cunningham drew in his breath as he took in the height of the vasty ceiling and then he walked over and looked at the things on the glass trolley . . . put out his finger to touch the battered stethoscope that still hung there.

'Your grandfather's?' he asked me and I thought I read pity in his eyes. I nodded my head and said nothing and then I set out on the by-now-familiar tour of the whole house and a silence settled on us. As I opened one door after another and saw their eyes probing all my loved belongings. The nursery was the last of all. I fixed my eyes on the dappled rocking horse in the corner and muttered with the self-possession of a five-year-old-child that it was a marvellous house for children. She tucked her arm in his and made a coquettish little movement against his side.

'Children! the girl says.'

She was making fun of me but I did not think he knew I existed. I turned towards him and began to mutter that if they wanted central heating put in there was a very good plumber in the village who was reasonable in his charges and that he was a patient too as they all were.

'The butcher, the baker, the candlestick-maker,' she said with her tinkling little laugh and the sun made a glory of her blond hair as she spun on her heel. 'How quaint! Are you still determined to turn your back on the fleshpots of Harley Street Johnny? You know what Pops said and honestly I can't see you sticking it out here.'

He paid her no more attention than he did me but went off down the landing and stood for us to pass him and descend the stairs and Annie was crossing the hall with the tea tray and I saw that she had been impressed enough by the white car to put out the Limoges china.

Presently we sat in the sitting room and I tried to make polite conversation but he was still very quiet and withdrawn. Then he noticed my trembling hands and smiled at me.

'I understand there is a slight possibility of buying the whole house, but if not at least the in-coming man could rent the surgery?'

Again I nodded my head and filled my mouth with one of Annie's sandwiches but it had developed the property of being chewed for an eternity but never swallowed.

'Would there be any objection if the in-coming

41

man wanted to carry out reasonable alterations in the surgery and waiting-room . . . redecoration for one thing and then perhaps a dividing wall to make a dressing room . . . a direct door through from the waiting room to the actual surgery . . . that sort of idea? It would be pretty difficult to do good work in there the way it is. The filing system is rather 'Heath-Robinson' and the heating is bad . . . the plumbing too. Of course I'd have my own equipment . . . desk exam. couch and dressing trolleys . . . all the usual kit . . . Things have moved a bit since your grandfather's day and I feel one owes it to one's patients to keep up to the minute. It's no good just muddling along . . . '

I got up and walked to the fire and there I swallowed my mouthful in one bolt and felt the anger rising in my breast against all these young doctors and middle-aged ones too who had dared to bring their women-kind along to probe into my private life.

'Grandfather did good work in that surgery,' I said and felt a lump in my throat as if the sandwich had rushed back there and stuck. 'He was doing good work there before any of us were born . . . and he didn't muddle along. He did the work himself and never pushed off his cases on the house-men at the Hospital . . . who are worked off their feet in this day and age. I know the house is old-fashioned but it's gracious. It's been ours for a very long time indeed and we've always loved it and been happy in it. If you want to move with the times you'd best build yourself a jerry-built villa with match-board walls . . . where you can sit behind warped doors in an over-heated fug and hear every noise the children make in the house next door . . . watch the wood for rot too. None of it is seasoned.'

I stopped up short then for I knew I was being unpardonably rude and besides much to my rage my eyes had filled with tears and he had seen them in the glass over the fire-place. He got to his feet with concern in his face but Fenella was laughing again.

'Children the girl says,' she trilled out once more. 'If you're so set on them as Miss Lister is, Master Cunningham, perhaps we *had* better get a hutch of some kind to keep the kids in it but don't let's get all intense and heated. Tomorrow is another day and with any luck in the world the committee will turn you down my sweet and I'll persuade you to stay in civilised country and not venture out into the wilds to be sniped at by the native population.'

She stood up as gracefully as a cat and tucked his arm against her side but still he watched me in the mirror and again I read pity in his eyes and was angry with him . . . and with myself too.

'We must get along poppet,' she smiled at me. 'Thank you for giving us such a delicious tea. We'll get in touch if the committee don't nobble the lad but I'm not really counting on seeing Dr Jonathan Cunningham's brass plate up in St Agnes What's-it. That old plate of yours has been polished till it's quite unreadable. Didn't you ever think of having it re-engraved or whatever it is one does to brass plates?'

I turned round and bit my nether lip and after a while I told her sulkily that the medical profession considered such a plate a badge of honour. I even managed to put the veneer of a smile on my face.

'After all it's been on the wall of Church House for a great many years.'

'Obviously so duckie and is that an advantage in this space age of ours? I'd have thought not.'

He was on the verge of apologising to me for her behaviour and that would never have done. After all they were to be companions for life and I was just an unimportant ship that was passing into the night. I moved towards the door and soon we were outside in the drive and I was envying the white gold of her hair afresh as she tucked the scarlet Italian silk scarf about her neck. He leaned across to look up at me and his eyes were dark with sadness.

'Thank you for letting us see the house and I thank you for the tea. I'll telephone you about the decision whether or no . . . and I can see it's been a happy house. One can always tell. It's a fine place to have been a child . . . a place you'd never want to leave. I'm sorry . . . '

Then they were gone and I stood and watched the white car curve away out of sight round the bend of the drive and I never thought to see Dr Jonathan Cunningham again. For that matter I had not much faith that he would even remember to telephone me the next day so I sighed and went back to finish the creosoting of the barn . . . and Sam and I got it done at last . . . ship-shape and Bristol fashion.

# 3

Now had come the day when the final meeting had been called by the Executive Council in Wentbridge and Dr Camps would be relieved of the burden that he had carried so willingly in covering our practice. His practice was in Agnes Magna, a prosperous village seven miles across the fen.

That morning he arrived at Church House as cheerful as ever for all that he had been working at pressure for many weeks. He let himself in by the surgery entrance and stamped his way into the kitchen to surprise me floury to the elbows with baking as I was.

'You'll make a damn fine wife for some young man one of these days,' he laughed, and opened up the oven door with a fine carelessness.

'They're not done yet,' he proclaimed. 'They want another five minutes.'

'Is that so?' I said, and told him to help himself when he thought the tarts were done to his taste.

Presently he removed a batch of raspberry tarts and another of blackcurrant tarts and turned them out for me with great expertise and then set about testing them, trying not to burn his mouth.

'I wish my wife could cook like you do,' he said, and sat down in great comfort at the kitchen table. I had a creamy cup of coffee waiting for him and he sipped this gingerly. Then he began to try one tart after another and meanwhile we discussed the cases. We were alone in the great kitchen and I reminded him that I was worried about Annie and I wanted his opinion on her. In the weeks following the funeral she had 'pined'. She would not admit that there was anything wrong but her appetite had vanished. She was having tummy pains too and I had seen her pressing her hand to her side and going for the 'bicarb'. She would wait till she thought she was alone and then get a glass of milk and pour herself half a cup . . . add a flat teaspoonful of sodium bicarb then wait for relief. I knew she was losing weight or thought I did. Her clothes hung on her these days. Her face looked drawn. She might be worrying about Louisa's baby . . . the whole house was. She grieved over my grandfather's death. As she said 'the house was like a tomb without him'. She had refused to let me tell Dr Camps anything about it.

'I don't know what nonsense you'll get in your head next. Poor Dr Camps has had enough to do without worriting about folk with nothing wrong with them. If Dr Robert were here I might ask him, and anyway I don't want to be packed off to hospital and that's the first thing they think of these days, X-rays and such-like nonsense and waste of money and time. I'll not see Dr Camps and that's final. A body can't be examined without her consent so you can mind your own business, Miss.'

After the surgery this morning Dr Camps had arranged to see Louisa for a routine ante-natal exam and she was another mule of a woman where 'other doctors' were concerned. One would have thought that there was no doctor but the one who had departed. Louisa just played awkward and she a trained S.R.N. asked me to stay with her and what on earth was all the fuss about? She was very matter of fact about a first pregnancy at forty-five! She must have known well it might have been hazardous but now she laughed at Dr Camps and asked him what he was getting up the courage to say to her.

'The baby's lying right,' she said. 'We all know that. My blood pressure is like a young woman's. I've got no trace of albumen. I don't want to go up to Maternity and well you know it so don't suggest it now.'

'I'd like you to go in there for the

confinement, Sister, just for forty-eight hours and straight home again.'

'And why, Dr Camps? The old doctor promised me that he would bring this baby for me. He delivered me aged nought and *there's* nought and nothing wrong with me only that I don't like hospitals and sergeant-major sisters.'

'I know very well, Sister, that you and my colleague had a bargain between you that if the slightest thing went wrong you would agree willingly to be admitted at once.'

'But there's nothing to go wrong, Sir, now is there?'

'I'll not argue with you, Louisa. The new man will take you on and his will be the decision. He'll not take any risks with this baby, none of us can dare to and you'll not expect us to. You're not a fool.'

Louisa could not judge what was right.

'There's Sam,' she argued. 'I can't leave Sam. You know I've got to get him up and dressed most days as if he was a baby himself.'

I laughed at her then and told her that I was well up to the care of Sam and anyway when she was lying in she couldn't look after Sam and the baby too. She was so obsessed with the struggle against having the baby in hospital that she had not even noticed that

49

her mother was very off-colour. Talking about colour Annie had a yellowness about her that I had persuaded myself was jaundice but one can imagine anything . . . Louisa went off to fetch her mother eventually and Dr Camps told me that he had been present at Louisa's delivery to help my Gramp.

'I can recall the night well. I gave her chloroform by rag and bottle but it was a difficult delivery. Poor old Bob didn't expect much joy but Louisa yelled as soon as she arrived. I wasn't so long out of Medical School as I am now and I was never so glad ever since to hear a baby cry. Like mother like daughter. I wish that lady would get sense and now we have another like her. God have mercy on the new man, what's-his-name, young Cunningham. They don't know yet but my money is on him for the job.'

'Jonathan,' I told him. 'He seems to be a very reserved chap. They will perhaps be deciding it this minute in the Council Offices.'

I stayed on to help Annie get undressed and then I went back to the kitchen and found a batch of queen cakes burnt to a cinder through my not keeping my mind on my work in hand. I had an awful feeling in my breast that there was more trouble up ahead. I knew it when the doctor asked me to drive a

50

little way with him.

'I've got a visit in North Fen Estates bungalows. They're not numbered yet . . . not too sure of the way. Come with me, Lalage, and put me right.'

Of course I had known that Annie was ill. I had bullied her into letting Dr Camps see her. I knew now that he would tell me in private and this was his way of doing it. There were too many listening ears in Church House but out on the North Fen with his arm along the seat at my back I listened to what he told me . . . poor old Annie . . . almost certainly had a noxious growth in her stomach, a noxious crab-like thing that would grow outwards and spread in every direction and put her in her grave in the churchyard before the snowdrops came again. I listened to his voice telling me the awful things . . . listened as he added the balm that I had the heart of a lion and must be the strong one of the family. I knew I was not the strong one. I had come to the end of any reserve of any courage I possessed but I must not allow myself the luxury of weeping in his arms.

'Of course there might be another explanation for all these symptoms you noticed. She's had a great blow in the old man's death . . . and there's the strain of worrying about Louisa and her baby. It might be a nervous thing of no account whatever and that's what we must find out . . . and find out at once. That's what we must hope and pray for . . . but it's only a chance . . . and you must be prepared for bad news . . . and for pity's sake we must get this new man to talk Louisa into behaving with some modicum of common sense or you'll have another tragedy on your hands.'

He sighed and leaned down to start the car engine.

'I could find Bert Gawthrop's new bungalow in the North Fen Estate with my eyes shut as you well realise. It was the only thing I could think of on the spur of the moment to get you on your own. I'm sorry to have had to give it to you straight like this, Annie must be like a mother to you.'

I leaned back and closed my eyes and remembered my own mother. I could recall a soft velvet housecoat the colour of violets . . . and the scent of violets too . . . a pale hand that came out to light the little floating candle by my bed and a kiss that brushed my forehead like a butterfly. The sweetness of the memory was all I had of her . . . and my father had been as tall as a cliff in a black greatcoat with two gold wavy stripes on the sleeve of it . . . and a crimson stripe that ran between them. Annie had been my mother and my father and my sisters and my brothers. There was nothing I would not do for Annie and now she surely was condemned to unpleasant death. I felt the tears well through my lids and turned my head to look out through the car window so that he would not notice.

'We must pray very hard that it's not . . . what you think . . . and if it is we must make the time happy for her . . . see that Louisa's baby is well and strong. That's what she'll like best of all, isn't it? It will be like 'Now lettest Thou Thy servant depart in peace',' I whispered.

'You're a funny girl, Lalage, and your grandfather was right about you. You can carry their burdens and never know the weariness of it . . . at a time when you should be laughing and loving and having babies of your own . . . and talking about that reminds me of this Cunningham chap. They came on to me after they'd seen over Church House. That fiancée of his is a real eye-opener for a start.'

'Fenella,' I said and he laughed and said the name suited her.

'If he's the chosen candidate — and I'll put my money on him — are you going to sell him the house?' he asked me. 'The decision should have been made by now.'

I thought of the old misery which had been thrust aside by fresh ones. My thoughts were rats in a trap from which there was never an escape.

'I haven't decided. I'd like to stay on here indefinitely but it's difficult.'

Difficult was not the right word. I should have said impossible and had done with it. James John had been badgering me to make up my mind for there was very little money coming in and I had not found employment, not that I had tried very hard. I had no specific training. Nobody wanted a young woman who could cook and sew and run a house and go home at night but then I had not tried. I had put off the decision from one day to the next and painted the barn but there was no putting it off past today.

By now surely the new doctor would have been appointed. I watched the rain slanting down out of the sodden sky and the willows lashed obliquely by the wind. I hardly listened to what Dr Camps was saying. Then he got to the subject of Dr Cunningham's fiancée again.

'Fenella won't be much support to a struggling young G.P.,' he said. 'You'll have to take him under your wing for you know the ropes, none better, especially if she believes what I told her myself. I had no mad desire to have every second week-end free. When my work is finished then my free time starts. It's far too late to teach an old dog new tricks. Besides I couldn't have that young man coming on my practice and diagnosing all the mistakes I've made in the last ten years.'

I had to smile at that for it was far more likely that he would not trust his beloved patients to the tender mercies of a less experienced man than he was himself.

'A doctor can't work from ten till six, my dear. It's when the darkness comes down that fear begins to rise up in the human heart . . . and it's no good sending for a stranger to sit by the bed of an old friend when he sees his last sun go down. God never afflicted His creation of man with convenient diseases that occur on Tuesdays Thursdays and Saturdays and never on the Sabbath Day. I know I'm old and foolish and maybe near retirement one of these days but I believe that medicine is a noble profession . . . and by God there's a reward to it too. A man can feel like a god when he's only a humble instrument in God's hand and it's a good way to feel. It's a tragedy you never got the chance to fulfil all those dreams of yours. You can understand what I'm talking about . . . when most of your generation would think me 'sans everything' like Shakespeare had it and do me that favour like a good girl, take that young man under your wing . . . just to oblige me.'

I reminded him that Dr Cunningham had not yet been appointed and he laughed me to scorn.

'Old Brown of Cotton is chairman of the committee and he's a pompous old ass like myself but he knows a promising chap when he sees him. They'll elect the boy without a doubt if he has the sense not to introduce the fair Fenella to the meeting . . . He may be fool enough to bring her along too for I suppose he sees no fault in her if he loves her. Now that I think of it it didn't strike me that he loved her all that much. There was something missing in the way he looked at her when she said some of the more foolish things. His eyes weren't the eyes of a young man in love . . . but perhaps I'm not such a good witch doctor as I think I am. By God! She asked me why 'old Lister' didn't have his brass plate polished in a foundry . . . so that it couldn't be read. Was she off her head do you think?'

There was no possible doubt that Dr Camps was a very excellent witch doctor as indeed I found out later in the day. I spring-cleaned the surgery and the waiting room very thoroughly just to keep my mind off the fact that in the town thirty miles away they would be deciding the fate of the patients who had come to Church House all the years I remembered. It was such an important thing for the whole village that the right man would get the position. I finished at last and wondered if the meeting were over yet. I longed to pick up the phone and ring the office but I knew it was no business of mine now. It would be a presumptuous act on my part. I went upstairs and changed into a pair of dark jeans and a green high-necked sweater that James John once said made my eyes like emeralds from Guatemala. I brushed my hair for a hundred strokes and remembered that Annie had one chance in a hundred of being alive this time next year. I pushed back the possibility that she would die . . . the possibility that anything might happen to the new baby. I concentrated on winding the two heavy plaits up in a high coil on the top of my head. Jonathan Cunningham had said he would ring me whether or not he was successful at the interview and at the other end of the line he would not see my eyes and think they were like emeralds from Guatemala . . . and what if he did? I dusted my nose with powder and wished that it was a little patrician nose like Fenella's and did not turn up at the tip . . . wished I had a white mink coat and a car to match . . . wished that a deal of trouble was not rolling towards Church House on the conveyer belt of time.

The telephone by the bedside almost made me jump out of my skin and it was the boy at the National Health office in town . . . the friendly one with the fair hair who had always brought me in and given me tea if I waited for Grandfather to be finished with his meetings.

'Good afternoon, Miss Lister. The Great White Chief wants to talk to you personally. Can you hold the line a moment please?'

So the Clerk of the Executive Committee was going to tell me the result of the interviews. I hope that my heartbeats were not as audible in the office in Wentbridge as they were in my own ears.

'Hello there, Lalage. I thought you'd like to know we've appointed the new man. After all who has more right than you to hear the result? I don't know if it'll surprise you. You met our hopeful candidates and you knew the ones on the short list . . .'

I wanted to ask him who it was but I forced myself to thank him for the kindness he was showing in letting me know so soon and we talked polite little words for a hundred thousand years and then I had it . . .

'We gave it to young Cunningham. I expect you remember him . . . chap with black hair . . . saw you yesterday afternoon and liked the house very much. Dr Brown took a great shine to him. They all did . . . seems the right type for country practice. His father was a G.P. and his grandfather too . . . and a straight boy too. He knew we were determined to have a married man and he blurted it out to us even before we gave the decision . . . got very awkward about it and no wonder. He'd broken off his engagement with his lady last night, I don't know the ins and outs of it but he was frank enough to tell us about it *before* and not *after* the decision. He says he has no prospects of marriage any more and apologised for wasting our time but it only just happened old Brown asked him if he did not think he would get married after a year or two . . . tried to put it in his mouth to say yes, but Cunningham wouldn't have it . . . said it would be unlikely but that didn't mean he would not work to the best of his ability and try to match up with the Lister tradition . . . believes in medical tradition apparently . . . and of course wife or no wife they gave him the post.'

My heart was still pounding in great beats up into my throat though I could think of nothing to explain it. I had expected Jonathan Cunningham to be elected after what Dr Camps had said.

'He's on his way out in his car to see you now . . . should be almost there by this. I hope you'll help him all you can, Lalage. Let's hope he measures up to the last of them all . . . '

I walked slowly down the graceful curve of the staircase and wondered if Jonathan Cunningham was as unhappy as I. He too had lost the one he loved best and in a far more painful manner . . . without the dignity and the finality of death. There must have been a scene and recriminations. They would have said ugly harsh hurtful things to each other, perhaps not meaning them . . . only seeking to wound. I sat by the fire in the sitting-room with my hands in my lap like any lady of leisure and waited for the sound of the white car in the drive. Dr Camps was gone but he had left a written message for the incoming doctor . . . he had read it out to me . . . See Louisa as soon as maybe? Hospital delivery. Aged Primip also urgent investigation on Annie — ? cachectic disease. Will telephone you tonight Lalage knows picture.

I even tried not to get up to look out through the window when I heard the engine but failed to resist the temptation and I was disappointed suddenly for it was not the white car after all but a sports Daimler of uncertain vintage . . . a long low rakish car too and it was worth all of twenty-five pounds. I let out my breath with a great sigh and knew the white car had been Fenella's ... the riches had been Fenella's ... the luxury hers too. By the look of the noble 'old banger' Jonathan Cunningham was as poor as ... myself. I crossed the carpet and sat down again decorously and waited till Louisa came in to announce him ... and a great awkwardness descended on the room that I was at a loss to understand. Of course the broken engagement was an embarrassment. I stretched out my hand to shake his and he looked down at it for an instant before he took it and the moment when Fenella had refused to shake my grubby paw stood between us like a physical thing.

'It's hard to get the creosote to scrub off,' I apologised and he smiled at that and hoped that I hadn't made any more swift descents from my ladder.

'You know about the appointment, Miss Lister? They said at the office they'd ring through.'

I saw too late that I should have congratulated him instead of muttering about the state of my hands and I did so now awkwardly and belatedly and knew that I compared badly to the gaiety and the poise and the glamour he obviously sought in a woman. I went on from bad to worse for I was as forthright as James John was for not mincing words.

'I heard about your engagement too . . . that it's broken I mean . . . and I'm terribly sorry. If there's anything I could do to help . . . go to see her or something though I'm not very good at persuading people . . . or anything but I could try . . . '

I stuttered on and on for a full minute and he glanced at me in surprise at the thought of my acting as an intermediary.

'You're actually offering to see Fenella and soften her heart for me . . . on such very short acquaintance too. Oh, no, Miss Lister that's the last thing I'd send you to do. That's over and done with and best forgotten but I thank you most sincerely. Everybody has been telling me you're a lassie of many parts and everybody calls you 'Lalage'. I expect I'll find myself calling you 'Lalage' myself sooner or later. Would you object if I started straight away?'

I shook my head and went over to pour out the tea and was glad they had sent in the Limoges china again and once more I discovered the phenomenon of food that would be chewed for an eternity and not swallowed as we progressed from one difficult topic to the next.

'I've been speaking to your solicitor about the renting of the surgery and I think the terms are very fair so I'll become your tenant from today if you agree, and there's the question of the house. Your lawman said you'd not made up your mind but I'm afraid I couldn't buy it from you no matter how much I'd like to. It's the sort of a background I'd like to have for my children and for my children's children . . .'

Between us again Fenella stood like a small wraith and whispered 'Children, the girl said'.

'It's a long and complicated story but I'll abridge it. Bryan said you were used to listening to other people's hard-luck stories . . .'

It seemed that his parents were dead and any capital they possessed had been eaten up in his father's last prolonged illness. The usual way of raising the money to purchase a house was by life insurance and Jonathan Cunningham's life was not insurable. There had been a car accident and fractured ribs and lacerated lungs . . .

'Don't think I'm an invalid. I expect I'll live as long as the next man but you know insurance companies . . . so there's no capital . . . ergo no house . . . I have some rather fine relatives . . . aunts and uncles and cousins. The family is in steel and my branch of it is the only one that ever took to doctoring. There was a great-grandfather a long time ago who was foolish enough . . . in the eyes of his father . . . to become an apothecary and his son had no more sense than he had . . . or his son's son. Then I failed to see myself as a big business tycoon too . . . '

He gave me a faint apologetic smile and reminded me that he had warned me it was a long story and then he went on again rather haltingly, stopping sometimes as if he considered what to say next.

'I finished at University and at Medical School. Then I had this accident. I didn't bring it upon myself, I assure you . . . got involved in an argument between a double decker bus and a lorry and came out of it the worst of them all . . . like many a man who interferes . . . '

Again he smiled the same shy deprecating smile and bent his head to watch the flames leaping up the throat of the chimney.

'I had been rather proud of my physical proficiency so I was like Lucifer Prince of the Morning. I took a toss from the heights and I lay on my back for a year or two with lung involvement. One side had taken it rather badly . . . caved in a bit but they got it pulled out again. When I was better I tried to get a few extra letters after my name. It was that pride of mine again I suppose . . . I took a job in the north too . . . industrial practice and rather busy. I'm afraid I was too ambitious. I had studied during my illness and I burnt the midnight oil a bit and was invalided out again . . . only six months this time. The sum total of all this was that I was told to seek a quiet rural practice . . . '

So that was the reason for the drawn look about his eyes. His sun tan did not mean winter sports after all but ultra violet light in hospital physio departments. There was silence in the room except for the ticking of the clock on the mantelpiece and I smiled at him and told him that St Agnes Parva could certainly be regarded as a quiet place.

'People regard it as being too quiet. If you're looking for sanctuary you'll find it here. The Harvest Festival is the high spot of the year not counting Christmas Day. They'll expect you to read the lesson in Church on Sundays. Grandfather always did but if he was out on an emergency Sam Frazer, Louisa's husband, filled in. Louisa wheels him up to the lectern and he reads well. My grandfather often pretended to have a call just to give the Bo'sun a chance to do it just to show off a bit. He's got disseminated sclerosis. I think you saw him yesterday.'

He looked at me thoughtfully and then

turned his face back to the blazing logs.

'He was a great man, Robert Lister. I hope I won't be a bitter wind of change . . . 'a bitter thing for a shorn lamb.''

He paused for a long time before he went on haltingly.

'So I've explained why I can't buy the house. I'll have to get rooms somewhere in the village. I'd like to have had it but you'll maybe find me a berth in one of the houses hereabouts. Do you know anybody who would be willing to put me up?'

I set down my cup on the tray and tidied the things quite unnecessarily. Then I leaned forward with my elbows on my knees, a hand shading my face and the thoughts went off in my head like jumping crackers . . . like rockets that soared up into a night sky.

He could not possibly know that there was no chance of my keeping on the house though I had tried hard enough. I must sell to the highest bidder. Then Annie might have to die in a strange house. Louisa's baby would never know the joy of the cherry orchard in the spring . . . nor what it was to soar almost to the clouds on a summer day on the old garden swing . . . never know the glory of the American Pillar Rambler Rose on the long trellis on a June day . . . nor what a magic place the house became on Christmas

Eve . . . It must all go . . . vanish into the future. It would be chopped about and turned into a legion of little flats. The garden would be covered with a rash of red-brick bungalows. A tractor would come one day and plough across the smooth grass and tear up all the lovely old trees as if they were so many decayed teeth. I would have the rent of the surgery of course but it would not cover the running of the household . . . no matter how careful we were and we had learned to be very careful indeed. Sam's pension would provide for the Frazers . . . for Annie too but there were rates and taxes. There were repairs and renovations. I had learned to type in the last few weeks in an effort to make myself more employable but I would never be any good at it without a deal of practice and there just was not the time left. I could never hold down a secretarial job . . . not for a year or two . . . and Annie must not die . . . if she had to die . . . she must not have to set out on that dark voyage from a strange room in a strange house . . . an unfeeling new unfriendly house . . . and I had to find her wages no matter how she complained about it. Although she knew nothing about it I had sold some of my mother's jewellery and known myself a traitor for doing it. I had got next to nothing for it too and I knew I should

67

never have parted with it. I had so little of her that every smallest piece was more precious than anybody would ever know.

Yet there must be some way to bring in a small regular income . . . and this young man wanted lodgings . . . two rooms perhaps and meals. The house was enormous and whatever about my typing proficiency at least I could cook adequately. I felt the crimson tide flood up from my neck to my face and felt just as I had done in the Wentbridge jeweller's shop with Mother's ruby necklet trickling through my shaking fingers. I could not stop my hands shaking now but I hoped he did not notice it and still I hid my face from his eyes.

'If you liked . . . if you thought it would be all right for you . . . but perhaps you wouldn't . . . I could . . . we could . . . oh dear how can I put it? This house . . . is big enough . . . too big. We have plenty of most willing hands. You could stay with us . . . have your own separate sitting room . . . if you wanted . . . if you wanted to study. We could give you full board . . . and you'd be most welcome . . .'

I felt like an impoverished gentlewoman interviewing her first paying guest and indeed that was just what I was and I stumbled on and on till finally my words wound down to a small whisper.

'So if you liked . . . we could put you up here . . . but if you'd feel happier with strangers . . . though of course we'd be strangers too . . . you could stay . . . here and you'd never be strangers — not in this house . . . not to us.'

There was silence in the room when I had finished and still I sat forward with my elbows on my knees and still I shaded my face from his gaze and I wondered why I had lost all sense of social behaviour . . . just because I had to offer full board and lodging to Dr Jonathan Cunningham, the newly appointed doctor in the village of St Agnes Parva.

I am not quite clear about what happened next. Jonathan stopped his study of the fire and got to his feet.

'You'd allow me to live here in the Surgery House . . . in Church House itself? I could live here as if I were family and we'd have a Bo'sun who could read the lessons on Sundays . . . and his wife an S.R.N . . . Sister Louisa was a Queen Alexandra and she was Sister on a troop ship . . . can do nursing and reception . . . and old Annie in the war could be quartermaster . . . and the Admiral Benbow Inn . . . I've been so curious about it. The Clerk of the Executive told me it all. All I know is that the Bo'sun and you paint the old barn with creosote when the sea runs into storms. I accept any terms you make, Lalage.

Arrange it all with James John your attorney. I'm not haggling with yourself. I'll play fair with you.

'If you knew what it will mean to me to be part of a family again . . . you'd not believe it . . . '

My brain was running over like a ticker tape . . . James John would see to it on the business side. If Louisa would take the position as receptionist and I had income as a landlady for board and lodging for him. There were new rules in the N.H.S. Fees could be claimed for ancillary workers . . . secretaries and nurses but now Jonathan wanted to see the Admiral Benbow Inn. Its fame had gone as far as the National Health Office in Wentbridge. He seemed to know all about it. I think we all trooped out together. He had a magnetism that gathered us up like a magnet might attract tin-tacks. Certainly the Admiral Benbow stopped him up short. He stood opposite the model of the *Victory* and took a deep breath. I saw his eyes go down to the intention tremor in the Bo'sun's hands and sadness about him yet he laughed as he heard again the tale of the blow-lamp blitz of the cordage. Annie was fussing over the tortoise stove, opening up the damper and feeding it with ash wood from the fen. Louisa had put the Primus on and got the sherry bottle out and the Bovril. The kettle had started to sing and I knew the hospitality of the Admiral Benbow by this. The 'new doctor' was lost in his own thoughts, not taking any notice of the multiple conversations. Maybe he saw what a paradise it could be. Jonathan looked at the intention tremor again and set himself to the point in hand. It was the first time I saw him as the miracle man in 'the passing of the third-floor back'. It was not to be the last time. He had a mug of sherry and Bovril in his hand by this and was sipping it carefully and with enjoyment.

'I have a family in business, not that I ever joined it . . . an uncle in the north who is hungry for labour seeking for ill people who cannot go to work. This uncle of mine is a good chap. He brings work to them and says they are the best there are in these days. This is the set-up for it. There's room and to spare at the far end of this barn . . . room going a begging. You could do him a favour, Sam. He sends out engineering work all over the country. God knows he has a fleet of vans coming out once a week or so to collect and they return at the end of so much time and they collect. It's no charity. You get a cheque in a week or so. It's not chicken feed. It works out to good wages. Mostly it's T.V. parts. If you can turn out this sort of thing, Bo'sun, you'd do it on your hands. These firms are hungry, starving for good labour. What do you think?' He took the *Victory* with a smile. 'If you could make that vessel twice!!!'

It was a miracle out of a magician's hat. It became the accustomed thing to see the van arrive to load the finished goods and collect the work articled . . . and always the cheque that made Sam the Bo'sun a working man again. Sam had a changed manner about him. He was an employed man and now he could add his pull to the effort. He turned out an extraordinary amount of work. Always on Fridays there was a van waiting for more and the cheque came back on time . . . and they wanted more and more and more.

But that's running ahead a bit. That first night we saw Jonathan to his quarters . . . the Master Bedroom, the telephone by his bed . . . the speaking tube to the front door. I gave him his own sitting-room which had been Gramp's library. We all worked at it. We got it ready before the evening. Jonathan's things could be sent on later. Tonight he had taken his new position and Sam had given an extra polish to the grate in the Library as we had always called it. The fire was winking and blinking and the ink was fresh in the ink-wells. The old copper bed-warmers were on the walls and each a sun in its own right . . . the copper kettles and the coffee pots and beer mullers. They were all there still. Yet Jonathan, God bless him, stopped by the long dining-room and hesitated . . .

'I thank you all very much but I'd prefer to eat with the family if you could put up with me. I've been very lonely.'

So we welcomed him in and set a place at the head of the table for him which he thought a great honour and after we had finished supper we went along and sat in his study and he entertained us royally and we all talked ourselves to exhaustion but nobody said a word about Fenella. I hoped she was not very unhappy by herself and I worried about the fact that he never mentioned her.

At last I asked him about her, hoped she would not be unhappy. He grinned at that and told me she was never unhappy but he agreed that she was a super girl although there was small chance he would love her till he died. I was not to worry about her nor yet about him. It would all come out in the wash. Then he took to laughing at me and I could not see why and Annie was put out with him and said he was like all the other men. It was the same with young people these days. It was off with the old and on with the new . . . and the Almighty knew we were probably all going to perdition.

# 4

These first days I did not realise the pin-pricks that would come nor how sharp they would be. I was surprised every time I found myself out of humour at the sight of Jonathan sitting behind the surgery desk, sitting at the head of the dining-table, smiling across the mahogany, walking up the aisle at church to read the lesson at the lectern in a formal dark suit. At home I would watch him taking the stairs two at a time and I knew I was a dog in the manger of the meanest sort. Jealousy was a cruel emotion and I was jealous. For one thing there was a full surgery attendance just to have a look at him so Louisa said for there was nothing wrong with any of them. He had asked her to sit in on surgeries to help him. Louisa was smart in her white coat and the room was packed. Jonathan had wanted me too. I sat on a tall stool at the long counter and tried to whip the list into some sort of order. I arranged the panel cards and I knew the task well. I set them like a dressing of soldiers along the counter in a file of dragoon guards. We had never been

74

too particular about regimentation. A proper receptionist would have seen that it was run with panache but I did not recognise the word yet.

I was as jealous as a green-eyed cat. The patients had no loyalty, it seemed loyalty had gone. This practice was my birth-right. Jonathan had collected it from under my nose. It was his now. It was finished and there was a jollity in the big surgery because of the wind of change that blew through it. I knew I came near to hating the conqueror. Everybody was glad to see him. My grandfather was forgotten and there was an eagerness and a great curiosity.

For all her advanced pregnancy Louisa had been pressed into reception. The Bo'sun came in later on and they discussed what I was to call the 'passing of the third-floor back'.

That morning I knew that Jonathan was fiercely given to crusades. A crusade was mounted already on Sam. In the weeks that followed Jonathan recognised the skill of the Bo'sun. Here was no ordinary labour. The Admiral Benbow had a strong bench. There was a kit to be issued gratis from the manufacturers. Jonathan picked out the skill that was born in the Bo'sun. A band-saw was important so a band-saw there was. The

Bo'sun was commissioned to cut out original templates from plans. He worked so accurately that he produced models for the other workers. It pleased him more than anything that he was a success. The 'boss' even asked him to sign his templates and there was a new dimension in the Admiral Benbow Inn and Bo'sun walked tall. He was his own man again even if his legs refused to carry him. What did it matter?

I overheard a secret conversation that morning between the doctor and Sam.

'You know that a regression happens an odd time. It's not incurable, this damn plague. It slings its hook and pushes off . . . slows down, eases up . . . maybe not a total cure but it slows to nothing. It's what doctors pray for. It is a possibility and one you must never forget. I've seen it happen.'

Jonathan looked at the bright wonder in Sam's eyes and spoke softly.

'Not often Sam, but it's possible. It's a matter of hope for us all . . . a matter for prayer maybe and faith . . . and in the meantime press on with those templates and good luck to you!'

It seemed a miracle how Sam improved from the very first. Jonathan certainly took an interest in Sam. I was well aware that there were Sundays when the doctor had urgent visits that were a fabrication that made the Bo'sun read the lessons in church. I would sit in our pew in the centre aisle and watch Louisa wheel up Sam's chair to the lectern and supervise the reading of the scriptures and there was something about Sam's readings that was pretty wonderful . . . 'and I saw a new heaven and a new earth' It was the wonderful seaman's diction of a Devon man . . . The former things had passed away something like that and the tears came to my eyes and I prayed inwardly that a miracle might happen. Surely God could cure Sam if He wanted to. He had just to stretch out His hand and touch him and he would be healed in that moment, but it might not happen as easily as that.

Jonathan would have taken himself off to the fen to get out of the way. I could imagine him out in Gibbet Fen direction. He had an interest in 'Squirrel Nutkin' and his jackdaw. I had told him about the way the boy had come to the funeral and occupied the hide in the chestnut tree, how he had left the wreath on the grave. The subject interested him very much. He was not a man to rush into any subject, but I knew he was watching for the extraordinary little character that I had described. There was a fen dyke that ran down the back land and passed near enough to Church House and the boy had a tub boat and the dyke was one of his kingdoms. I wondered sometimes if Jonathan visited Gibbet Fen on the look-out for the creature who lived wild on the fringe of the gypsy camp . . . of the gypsy people yet not of them . . . as wild as any hare.

The first surgery was crowded. Young Pegg came to get his wound dressed and collected some more mint toffees. We worked all the morning before we got near the finish and I had a feeling that we were in for prosperity. I agreed somewhere in the hours to take in the job of secretary and I was pleased to have the prospect of a salary that the N.H.S. would pay willingly. It seemed that Jonathan was doing his best to make us prosper and he cared.

He asked Louisa to keep up the position as receptionist but she tried to say no and he asked her if the work was too hard and she grinned at him and said that her figure was not what it had been. He refused to be amused and took it all too seriously. The joke died a miserable death and he frowned at her. 'So your smart uniform doesn't fit you any more Mrs Frazer? I don't know how you put such importance in things that don't matter a damn. You're completely and entirely camouflaged in that white coat. If you're worried about what the patients think of you I expect they are well aware that the abdomen enlarges in pregnancy. Besides that the village is full of expectant mothers. They won't be critical in the least of you. Come, Mrs Frazer, I want your help very badly. I'm a new boy at school.'

So Louisa was established at her own desk where she worked very happily and where she hummed to herself later on.

So there we are, Louisa and I in gainful employment but he had something up his sleeve for Louisa. We had no way of knowing that Jonathan had his lance levelled for another crusade. The last of the patients had gone and soon it would be lunchtime when the doctor said there would be just time for him to do Louisa's ante-natal exam.

Louisa got a shock but she girded herself against him, hands deep in pockets.

'Dr Camps checked me a few days ago. Everything is in order. I haven't time today. It's a waste of effort.'

Dr Camps always let her have her own way but she was not going to have it now. I knew that by the determination of his jaw.

'You do realise that I bear full responsibility for your case. I must see you professionally as soon as may be. Incidentally I want you to see to it that I see every expectant mother in the

79

next week or two. Set up extra appointments as maybe but you I will see now.'

She made a struggle like a landed fish and gave in without grace. I looked down at his gold signet ring as he palpated the abdomen.

'Now Mrs Frazer. There's been a battle about the idea of a hospital confinement. You must admit that you are an elderly primip. In this day and age hospital delivery is thought best.'

Louisa started off in her usual manner. I had heard her adopt it with Grandfather a time or two and later with Dr Camps. She would not leave Sam and anyway having babies was a normal affair. She would go in at the drop of a hat if things began to go wrong. I recognised it as whistling in the dark and she knew it too. He cut her off sharply and stood up like a silk, his lapels in his hands.

'Very well then, we'll have Sam in here at once if you please.'

She had no intention of having Sam in so she backed down a little but partial surrender was no good for him. I felt very sorry for her but I knew he was right.

'You're a trained nurse and I presume you've done your midwifery? You know what we're about here. Surely you'd not be the one to think of yourself first. You'd be the last one to do it. Don't forget the other people involved.'

He scowled across at her as if he did not like her one bit and I thought his words must strike fear into her.

'This baby is a pretty important individual. Boy or girl . . . it's Sam's whole future. You know the whole picture of the Bo'sun . . . what future he may expect and it's a bloody mean ending. In six years he'll be on his back in bed with far less muscular power than he has now . . . incontinent, still smiling mark you. You know the way it runs down. God have mercy on a gallant seaman. He didn't deserve it in the Battle of the Western Approaches . . . any more than his skipper deserved to drown. Give us six years and the wheel-chair will be a thing of the past. It will be some sort of benison if Sam possesses a little child to sit by his side . . . tell him the news of the house. Lose this child for him, Sister Louisa, and you'll destroy him.'

There was a horrified silence in the big room and I wished Annie would ring the gong for lunch. I could catch the faint aroma of toast and knew that Annie was finishing the last touches.

'You've got hospital phobia. All along you've made every excuse under the sun. You want the child born in Church House and

81

you're determined to run your own lying-in period. You'll have no chance of it if you're my patient. You'll do what you're told and you'll jump at it.'

It did not go on much longer. I huddled down into my shoulders and pretended I was not listening. Louisa had lost all her fire and I thought she seemed to have turned into a small child who had had her bottom spanked. There was a heart-broken air about her as if she felt that nobody loved her any more. She was making up to him as if to try to win favour. She made him smile and succeeded and his smile was quite the most pleasant thing about him. I had studied it by now, how it started with a deepening of the lines beside his mouth and progressed to laughter wrinkles by his eyes. His face lit up with merriment.

'I'm sorry to have been such a worry, Sir. I hate hospitals and I get homesick for Sam and the place here and the practice and Lalage and Mum. I have a phobia that if you go into hospital you may never come out again . . . never confessed that to anybody but it's confessed now. Forgive me. I'll do what I'm told. I expect I'd better go in to Maternity for a check up at any rate and we'll go on from there.'

'Thank you Sister.'

He liked her now. It was written all over him and he told her that he had not forgotten Mrs Tiplady and that was Annie. To his mind Louisa was a hard nut to crack but Annie was another and she could not be left. It was being arranged and there would be no trouble.

'If it's any trouble I think it's just a mental thing. She's had overmuch worry. Don't make any diagnosis till you have to, Sister, and I'm sorry for calling you Mrs Frazer like a minute gun. I was bullying you.'

The brassy reverberation of the gong for lunch carried along the surgery passage and Annie dished out her usual excellent steak and kidney pudding. Her cooking was its usual perfection but she did not fancy any herself. She did not appear at the dinner table except to serve and Louisa was absent too. Louisa had had a terrible shock as Annie explained it.

'What if she hadn't had her clean chemise on, she'd not have been able to look the doctor in the face till the end of her days.'

We lunched, Jonathan and I, and talked companionably together mostly about the strange gypsy boy that I called Squirrel Nutkin. Jonathan had not seen him yet but he was eager to look up his history notes. I thought Gramp had done everything possible for him. He was not considered educable. They had carried out all sorts of investigations but they had come up with nothing. He never spoke but he was not deaf. The hospital had taken him in for a time but it was not possible to hold him. They had given up trying. It was cruel. He was a wild thing and he was happy . . . There were notes in his panel card . . . a thick wad of them . . . an hour's reading I told Jonathan, as much as I remembered the findings of research. He had a dragging left leg and a low intelligence quotient yet he was as smart as a fox. His teeth wanted attention. They were broken and should be seen to. His hair was scanty. He lived by himself in a tarred fen hut near the gypsy encampment.

Jonathan looked across at me finally and told me that he had never had better steak and kidney pud. I was to congratulate Mrs Tiplady and to tell her that she had an appointment to see him professionally the next day. It would be convenient for him if she would stay on in bed in the morning. He would come to her room and examine her.

He smiled at me and told me that she could then put on a clean chemise if she thought it essential and this sort of thing was important to elderly ladies.

Mrs Tiplady, I thought. Nobody called her

anything but 'the doctor's Annie.' His message was like a bomb to Annie. I knew she would get no joy. She was determined that there was nothing wrong with her and she refused point blank to see him.

'She's not had a day's illness in her life,' Jonathan said to me, 'but Camps thinks she's malignant and she's as difficult as her daughter. Thank God I've found her Achilles heel.'

'Have you indeed?' I asked him and he smiled at me and I knew that none of us could ever prevail against him.

He looked at me straight in the eye.

'I will tell her that you have been crying in the night not because your grandfather is dead but because Annie is ill and you have noticed how ill she is. There is no doubt that she *is* ill and it is vital to have tests done at hospital as urgent. I'm not going to allow Mrs Tiplady the chance to raise a false alarm. If there's something wrong it will be put right. As a matter of fact I am setting up her appointments to visit Wentbridge Hospital as soon as maybe.'

He leaned across the table and took my hand in his.

'Take my word for it. It will all go through smoothly or so I hope. I'll drive her in to Wentbridge myself and you'd be very

85

welcome to come with us in case she jibs at the last moment.'

Of course there was a murderous row and we were all involved. At the height of it Annie declared that she was not going to strip for any whippersnapper of a young doctor and then she showed the frightened person she was when she chose to weep in my arms and surrendered.

'We'll face up to it then, Lally. That's what we'll do. Just come with me and hold my hand an odd time if it gets rough. It was not having the doctor himself any more. I had nobody to turn to and you but a child without kin.'

So the argument was resolved. Peace had come again to Church House and Jonathan and I were alone in the surgery and the surgery was finished for that evening. There had been a turmoil of emotions but now we were all set up for the next day. Louisa had taken herself off to help with the serving of the dinner and to talk soft words to her mother. Jonathan put his hands under my arms and lifted me to sit on the high stool and I was beginning to realise that my feelings for him were not those of a child. I knew well that this sophisticated young man found me of no interest whatever and he took himself off to the window to look out on the dark garden.

'About this business of Annie,' he said, 'we'll not have the end of the matter tomorrow nor the day after. Eventually we'll know but not right away. We'll get a straight X-ray and a full blood picture, a barium meal, a follow-through. At last we'll know it all but for a while we must wait. Now either it is or it isn't but it's like the thin red line . . . a battle for the courage to take it if it is. I want to say one thing to you, I'll not see her suffer. If it has to be done we'll bandage her eyes and forbear and bid her creep past. I promise you.'

I nodded my head and tried to picture the house without Annie and knew I stood on top of a precipice. I could in no way bear the thought of being without her. The thoughts piled in upon me of all the myriad small things that had built up that bound us so closely together. She would be hard up not to weep the days I went back to boarding school. She would be extra brusque and matter of fact as Gramp and she saw me off at Wentbridge station with my big trunk and tuck box. When the train pulled out of the platform I might weep but not if any of the other girls were there. It was not so bad after a year or two but the days I came home for holidays were like paradise. Church House would be heaven and the pantry full of my favourite things. Never would I forget the trolley in for tea by the fire. We always toasted muffins and the fire would be burning special logs that Annie had garnered on the fens. I could see her now armed for the harvest of ash. 'Ash warm and ash dry for the queen to warm her slippers by!' She had a trailer on the back of her bicycle and she would pedal the long miles of Smithy Fen. Gramp, Louisa, Sam. We would all be there for tea by the fire and they would listen to my brave adventures. Louisa and Annie made fine clothes for me so that I should not be outshone by the expensive clothes of some of my friends. I recalled the triumph when I got the silver swimming cup. Dear God! the visits to the dentist when Annie had nearly sickened me with cream buns afterwards to make it up to my trembling self.

'You were something far more special than a daughter to Annie,' Jonathan said. 'Please realise that I know now that you would gladly die for Annie and not count the cost. Don't think I don't understand.'

I had seen him work his skill with Sam and with Louisa, maybe with me. I knew maybe I was attracted to him but there was no future in it. He still loved Fenella.

He came back across the room and stood

opposite me and put his hand against my hair and stroked it.

'You know you're a very nice girl, Lalage. I don't know if I've met a finer girl. Even Fenella in all her glory was not arrayed like one of you.' And that was an odd thing to say.

I had typed out the list of visits for tomorrow and he picked it up and then turned back to me.

'I've drawn up my bargain with Annie and if you please you'll accompany us to the hospital tomorrow, not Louisa. Sister wasn't the one that noticed Mrs Tiplady was ailing and badly. You were the one that fretted about it. You're her small lost lamb and you rewarded her for all the effort of her life. You'd die for her this minute and think it an honour.'

I asked him how he persuaded Annie to agree to go for consultation and he smiled and he told me it was easy once he had found the key to Annie.

'I said that you had enough to worry you and it was no good her adding to your trouble. I *did* hear you crying in the night you know.'

So I had been the key to Annie. It seemed that he had taken the household by assault. I was very pleased that he had command. My heart sank with the thought of tomorrow all the same and I dreaded accompanying Annie to the hospital far more than she ever had dreaded my young dental adventures. I had a thrill of foreboding in the pit of my stomach and I had nightmares in the small hours so bad that I had to get up and throw cold water into my face to wake me out of terrors.

It was a brilliant morning once the sun came up. Annie was all dressed ready for the hospital with the big white apron and her Sunday hat perched on her head and speared with a hat-pin and a wisp of gauze over all. I tried to evade her and pick Brussels sprouts in the garden but she sent me upstairs to put on my overcoat.

'I don't have to be told that you've been gossiping with the doctor about me. Else you wouldn't have that daft look on your face nor be so white by half. It's all nonsense and a waste of everybody's time and don't say I didn't tell you so when it's all over.'

I said nothing. It was the best thing to do but she grumbled on at me.

'Dress properly when we go out in the car too. Those pants of yours haven't any warmth in them nor yet that cotton shirt. I don't see why you can't dress like a lady for a change. Look at Miss Fenella that the doctor brought here . . . dressed like a queen. You'll not see him looking at you if you don't smarten your ways a bit. A gentleman don't wed a girl with a backside like a lad's and her hair down in bows on her shoulders.'

After lunch I did the best I could with the black suit I had worn at the funeral. I put on a cream woollen sweater and pretended that my hair looked fine coiled up on the top of my head like Fenella's. It was no good. I was just not the same natural order as Fenella in her white mink coat and the red head-scarf. I could have done with a smart bag . . .

'You forgot your overcoat,' said Annie, 'but at least you put a skirt on yourself.'

Jonathan helped her into the back of the Daimler and muffled her up with rugs. Then he shoved me in the passenger seat and wrapped his coat round me. True enough it was bitterly cold but the heater soon made it warm and safe. There was a hum of power from the engine that was a memory of its mobility. After a while I turned round in the seat and tried to talk about Louisa's baby to take Annie's mind off her ordeal. She only looked at me out of her sharp periwinkle eyes — told me that Louisa was a daft ha'porth.

'I can't understand why a nice chap like Sam ever took up with Louisa in the first place. Please God the little old baby takes after her pa and not her maw. Takes after *her* pa that Louisa does, won't do a stroke of work if you're not after her all the time. Her paw was just the same. He used to scald my heart out of me but he's gone this long time, rest his soul.'

She closed her eyes and pretended to be asleep but I asked her if it was to be a boy or a girl.

'Reckon if it's not one 'twill be t'other,' she said sourly and turned her head to look out on the frost-gripped fields but I went on with it . . . reminded her that the daffodils would be out for the christening and we would stuff the church window niches with them . . . not the font. 'The font will be stuffed with the baby.' I tried a joke but she had no interest in it and I turned in my seat and closed my eyes. Slowly the tears ran one by one down my face and Jonathan began to talk to me in a voice that seemed calm after this fever of mine . . . Jonathan talked to me about quiet tranquil things.

The hedges would soon be getting on their tender green leaves. Every day now the sun would take 'a cock's step' towards light in the morning to spring. The whole world was turning to spring and all life was regenerating.

There would be snowdrops and aconites and crocuses and forsythia . . . and then the whole glory of it all . . . laburnum and lilac and all things bright and beautiful. The new lambs would appear and the ash buds all black in the front of March.

'It's strange the way the poets have it all. Tennyson had it. 'More black than ash-buds in the front of March'. He might have been describing your hair, Lalage.' I blinked my eyes open like a Dutch doll's with the surprise he gave me. Nobody had ever said such a poetic thing to me in my life before, not that I remembered.

Annie cleared her throat in the jump seat to demonstrate her presence there.

'Makes you look like a fairy princess that hair . . . hair as black as ebony and lips as red as blood . . . skin as white as snow . . . and talking of snow it does look as if we're in for snow. There will be plenty of it before the winter's done with us and we don't want any talk of snow,' Annie remarked kind of pointedly, but we were arriving into the edge of Wentbridge and soon we were turning into the hospital gates. Hostler had opened the gates for us and waved us through. He saw us to a parking place and they were expecting Mrs Tiplady. I was glad to hear that Hostler's bull terrier bitch had recovered from a distemper. The animal was an old friend of mine. She was the darling of Hostler's heart but she was given to

93

dog-fights and the murder of cats! She was satin smooth and so loving. There had been a time when I never went into hospital without a tribute to this Thurber dog. Hostler looked after Mrs Tiplady, accompanied us up in the lift and introduced us at the O.P.D. I clung to Annie's arm and wondered why she had got so grey and small.

The familiar antiseptic hospital smell enveloped me. Annie was handed over to the charge of a starched senior sister and led off. Jonathan grinned at me and told me that the darkest hour was just before the dawn and that it would soon be past. He steered me into the consultant's clinic and Dr James was an old acquaintance of mine. He started off a discussion of rugby with Jonathan that went on a long time. Then there was some talk about the practice and Annie. I settled into a small niche of my own and wondered what had become of Annie. Then she was back with a nurse and dressed in a white overall and a check dressing gown, very new slippers. She looked old and small and defenceless. She sat in front of the surgeon's desk and the questions were unending.

'But surely you wondered why you lost your appetite, Ma'am?

'And weight? Have you lost weight? Have

you noticed any blood? an issue of blood as the Bible says?

'Why didn't you come and see us at once? You were in a doctor's household. So the cobbler's child goes without boots?

'Is this pain of yours sharp in character or maybe gnawing?'

'It just wants a spoon of bicarb Sir. That puts it right most whiles.'

'Looking back over your life, say when your husband died did you ever lose a lot of weight?'

She was like a small ruffled bird as she sat upright on the chair and he told her she was a splendid old lady and I knew he was sorry for her.

I stood beside her in the cubicle and held her hand as he examined her and knew she was glad of my presence. Jonathan had gone away to look at the blood count. He came back presently and told me she seemed a bit anaemic, they would give her a few pints. I was stricken to the heart with the sight of the thin ribs and the wrinkled skin and the match-stick limbs. Of course there was something very wrong with her.

She must have been very tired with it all but she did not complain. The nurse was dressing her up now and making fun of the two spotless woollen vests and the whalebone corsets and the modesty vest pinned across her V-neck.

Then we were in a waiting room side by side on a wooden bench and we had wandered together into some awful nightmare from which there was no escape. We would sit in misery for the rest of eternity and Jonathan was gone again and might never come back and find us. The minutes dripped treacle into the unfathomable depths of time past and then quite suddenly the fair-haired sister was there.

'Will you come out and speak to the doctor, please, Miss Lister. 'I'll stay with the patient till you come back.'

I told Annie I would not be long. I was through the door and had shut it behind me. I leaned against it and let out a long sighing breath as I shut it behind me. If he wanted to speak to me alone he must have found something definite, Dr James. I was going to have the verdict. I turned my head and saw Jonathan coming along the corridor fifty yards away and I walked to meet him and my footsteps echoed from the flagged floor and the tiled walls and the high gloomy ceiling.

His face was filled with concern.

'Are you all right, Lalage? You look as if you're going to flake out.'

I could find no words to answer him. I

gazed into his face in an agony of entreaty that he would tell me what they had found. He walked me back along the corridor.

'Stay out here Honey. James wants to take Annie in as an emergency and I want to talk to Annie again without you. You'll side with her and nothing would be done. I've never lost a battle of words yet. You're too bloody kind. There is no doubt in James's mind or mine that she's for urgent admission. She's got no blood left and that's bad. James will admit her now and the bed is ready for her this minute but she has to say yes. I'll get it right. Make no error about that. It may take me a little persuasion but I'll see to it.'

Tonight she would have an urgent blood transfusion and tomorrow or the day after or the day after that all the terryfying investigations would start. They had come to no definite decision but it would come in time. It was possible that it was a false alarm but truth would out. There would be a detailed barium meal and a follow-through. It was on the cards they would find a growth in the transverse colon. On the other hand there was a hope that it was nothing. There was always 'anorexia nervosa' but Louisa was a worry to her and the old doctor's death had been a blow. But Louisa and her baby! Louisa was old to be a mother and it was not as if Sam was well. The blows had fallen on her one after another. It was a typical case of flesh not being able to carry the load.

I stood at the window in one of the dreary corridors when Jonathan had gone off to talk to Annie. I prayed.

Dear God. Don't let it be cancer. Even if it is that at this second of time make her whole again. It is easy for You. You know her goodness and all that's to do is to put out Your Hand. They say in the Bible that she would be healed from that moment. If ever You grant me a prayer grant me this. She believes in Your mercy and she taught me to believe in it too when they were all dying about us in the war years. Just don't send her down the awful slope of malignant disease. Let her enjoy the baby. She pretends it is not life and death to her but we all know she exists 'for the babby . . . for Louisa's babby' God. God. God. I promised Him all sorts of foolish things. I asked Him to give me the cancer and not her. I stood at a window and looked up at the pewter sky. 'I'll behave well to her and never tease her. I know there have been times when I have been wicked to her just to laugh at her old-fashioned ways. Never will I do it again. At this split second of time dear God show us Thy mercy.'

I did not go down to the Head Porter's

office. Hostler of the bull terrier bitch was watching for me. Jonathan came and found me at last as cheerful as ever I had seen him.

'She's gone up to the ward and settled in. We'll visit her later on to say goodnight.'

That was what we did. I asked him how he got submission and he said it was his secret. He put his arm through mine and we found her safely tucked in bed and not angry or resentful but very happy. I was happy that she had settled down and I kissed her goodnight and God bless. Jonathan insisted that we had dinner at Fitzherbert's as he had promised. It was a smart place much frequented by undergrads.

I swung up from the depths of depression to a high state of exhilaration. Suddenly I knew faith that my prayer was going to be answered. Jonathan was full of attention to me and teased me with ridiculous compliments.

He told me that he was the envy of 'every grad in the room' because 'Snow White' had taken dinner with him. He had a way of making me feel attractive and clever. Then we were in the car and evening was darkening into night and the street lights were on. He had wrapped his coat about me and tucked the rug about my knees and the heater was warm. The snow had started at last, not heavily but in drifting flakes now and again to be swept away by the wipers.

To my shame I slept now all the way home. I did not wake till he turned into the drive of Church House and I was very apologetic about it. Soon we were sitting together with fresh coffee and patum peperium on hot buttered toast and telling the others all that had happened. I seemed to have lost some of my shyness and my awkwardness where he was concerned and to behave like a rational human being.

The days that followed were very hectic. I drove into Wentbridge in Gramp's old car and visited Annie and found her better after the transfusion and I was happier than I had been for a long time. The practice was very busy but we found time to go skating for miles along the frozen fen reaches after the surgery when the moon was coming up the sky. Jonathan was very happy. He teased me with ridiculous compliments and I could almost believe they were sincere. Maybe I was falling in love with him. I admitted it to myself and knew it was folly. Then there was the problem of Louisa. I was given the task of ferrying her into Maternity to book in so it had to be the half-holiday and the Bo'sun looked after the reception and any emergency arising. Louisa and I had a great time in Maternity and poisoned our systems with tea in some of the wards. There was a place booked for hospital confinement unless it 'went like shelling peas'. Knowing the nature of midwifery there might not be time even for her to get in to Mill Road. If 'it' came quickly we must get on with it. Surely there were enough of us to deliver a baby in Agnes Parva but no risks must be taken. They all knew that and there might be chancy weather on the fens. It was one of the hazards. It happened an odd winter.

Louisa wanted a home confinement. There was no mistaking that but she was no fool. We must keep an eye on the weather and see how it turned out. The ambulance boys would have her in so fast that the time will beat the clock. 'The favourite place for delivery is the corner when they turn into Mill Road,' that's what Bill the ambulance man said so one of the night sisters had it.

It was killingly funny and we were all very amused at Louisa's baby. Louisa was plotting not to say a word about what she called 'contractions' till the baby was born.

I was losing my resentment against Jonathan's success with the practice. He was making a great many changes in the work and I sulked about it but only an odd time and now he took no notice of it. He had ordered new instruments and surgery equipment up from London. Some of the outmoded things were shifted out to the Admiral Benbow Inn and made very welcome there. The surgery had a new look and I knew it was seemly but I refused to be enthusiastic. I went out to the barn to view the old filing cabinets and I perched myself on the discarded couch and gave myself over to black thoughts. He sought me out.

'It's time you got the records transferred before the surgery hour or we'll be in a hell of a mess tonight. You and Louisa can see to it if you step lively now.

'You'll have to take the reception job when Louisa's off too. She may not want it when she's got a mother's chores to do. It's all for discussion.'

'Louisa was S.R.N. I've no training.'

He looked at me coldly and he was a different man from the one who had flirted with me in Fitzherbert's or out skating on the frozen fen reaches.

'For God's sake, you type the hospital letters, you sort out the cards, you wipe up the tears. The children come gently to your hand. I don't know what more you want to do. I prefer to do the diagnosis myself. By the way, Mrs Black said you told her that her child with the chicken-pox could attend school and he's still infectious.'

His eyebrows were lifted.

'I told her he wasn't to go back,' he added. 'No chance.'

He had me there and I got off the couch and walked back into the surgery and started to assemble the cards in a rush. He was not annoyed with me. He said if I accepted an ancillary's salary I must do as I was told but I thought he was very amused with the whole thing.

'Please explain why you issued wrong advice over my head.'

I looked down at the fresh tiled floor and knew it was a good job yet I told myself that the brick floor had been good enough for Grandfather. It had been Len Marshall's brother Bill who had done a rush job on the tiling and the painting and decoration too and Sam had helped. Louisa had been shop-steward self-appointed.

'The Blacks are very poor,' I said and Jonathan asked me if that excused the fact that I had infected the school with chicken-pox during the last three days.

'Jimmy isn't infecting anybody. The teacher knows that family by this. She will put him into a corral behind the harmonium and everybody will know not to go near him unless they want to collect a page of sums.

There's no fun at home for the poor chap and rarely enough to eat. Mother works on the land . . . jobs like pulling sugar-beet. She works hard but Black never works at all. Poor Jimmy needs that school milk. He gets a good hot dinner at school and if there's any left he has a second helping. He is warm and he's happy even behind the harmonium. My grandfather would have agreed with me.'

'Would he indeed?' he growled and then the phone rang on the desk at his hand and he lifted it up and told me it was the hospital, one of the probationers from Annie's ward. It seemed it was about Annie . . . something was up. I dropped a bundle of panel cards down on the floor and bent to retrieve them, listened to the voice on the phone, looked round to make sure that Louisa was out of the surgery.

'Yes I've seen you in Six and you're a patient of mine now. You do live in Agnes Parva.'

There was some more conversation and he said that Miss Lister would go at once. Sam Frazer would take the Daimler and be there soon unless the roads were worse. He asked to speak to Sister but there was hesitation and it sounded as if that was not possible. There was a long pause and he glanced at me and told me that it could not be discussed at

104

telephone level and that there was something odd going on. Then the phone clicked off.

He came across to the table and sorted the spilt cards to help me. Then he was back at the phone and dialling the phone annoyed and more annoyed when he waited and found it engaged and engaged and engaged.

'Annie's dead isn't she?' I whispered and he said he did not think so but it was very odd.

'That's a brand new probationer. She'd not be let use the phone at all and certainly with any message of importance but she did say there was enough trouble already and drive slow.'

For some reason not far from tears I said I was sorry about Jimmy Black and he told me not to worry about it. 'Dr Lister never made errors about things like that, Lalage, and I don't want to have Louisa in on this . . . don't let her hear about the call nor that Sam is taking you in the car. I'll ring from the hospital and contact her with the news as soon as I can get some reason out of them. Louisa can stay and help with the surgery and we'll start it as soon as you and Sam are away. There's an urgent case on its way in with the police. I'd have gone with you myself only for it.'

He found Sam and appeared at the car with him in the chair. It took him a very short time to load the chair into the jump-seat after he had lifted Sam behind the steering wheel. I was in the passenger seat and so bundled in rugs that I could hardly know what went on. I disentangled myself and heard Jonathan speak softly.

'Quietly now Bo'sun. Take it steady over the gravel and mind how you go on the roads. Good luck to you both. Take care.'

He ran a few steps after us as the car moved off.

'I'll ring Hostler at the hospital and have him meet the car to help with the wheelchair . . . get more definite information if I can . . .'

I waved him goodbye and then we were safely out of the gates. Then I tried to tell Sam exactly what had happened.

'The little probationer rang Jonathan. There was a flap on in the hospital about Annie. She was all muddled up and he couldn't make sense of her. At any rate it was an emergency and it was Annie. Honestly Sam, I don't know what to think but Louisa mustn't know anything about it so she has to carry on with surgery. They have a police case coming in tonight. I do know that. It's seems there's big trouble on with Annie in Wentbridge. The young nurse on the phone was at the end of her tether. It was all her

106

fault what had happened to Annie. We don't want Louisa involved so she won't be told. We'll ring back as soon as we know anything definite. Louisa will have the police in tonight with Mrs Black and not because of this chicken-pox scare . . . just because she has had some panties stolen off her clothes line in the yard. Oh, Sam, you know the gossip in a practice as well as I do. Mrs Black is a wrong 'un. There's all this fuss about Jimmy and his chicken-pox and I'm in big trouble about this with the boss. Now Mrs B has come up with somebody pinching the clothes off her line and with a tale about a man who has attacked her in the night hours for 'carnal knowledge'. 'It were over by the cut,' she says.

'That's woman's gossip,' Sam said. 'Forget it and don't worry none. Tell me about tonight.'

I went over it again, the strange call from the hospital. 'It came from a probationer on Six and that's Annie's ward. She's from Agnes Parva and I know her, Bo'sun. Her name is Wendy Nightingale. She's often nearly out of her mind with fright. The hospital takes a bit of getting used to after Agnes. I think she was trying to tell us that Annie was ill. She asked that Miss Lister come in as quick as possible. Hospitals are not so gormless as to put her on the switchboard for messages.'

'Hospitals are always gormless,' said Sam and grinned at me to keep my spirits up. 'Please God Louisa doesn't know this lot till it's all over. Don't be frit about this road. It's the same old dyke road that never changes. In hard weather it's edged by two drowning channels and I've driven it a time or two and never drowned yet. As for the little nurse to my mind there's damn all wrong but some woman's row. Women in hospital are fighting cats and if I was you I'd not worry. Worry kills cats. If there's a row on leave it to Hostler. He'll call his bull terrier bitch. She's a great one at killing cats.'

The fen was lovely in the moonlight with the moon queen of it all and the road powdered diamond.

'I have a feeling that this is a false alarm,' Sam went on. 'We'll not fire till we see the whites of their eyes.'

'Louisa knows nothing about it,' I said. 'She's all wrapped up by now with Mrs Black and the knickers stolen off her line. That's a nice thing to happen in Agnes Parva.'

Sam was determined to keep me unworried so he told me that the crime of knicker-larceny was very common on the fens because little boys grew up too fast.

He dared me not to smile as he went on.

'They settle down when it's worked out of

108

them on the sugar beet.'

'It's out in the village that she's alleging rape. Black's spread the news over the King Bill that his missus can't keep her drawers on the line and it's all bull-shine.'

'And that's rude,' I reproached him . . . 'to talk like that with poor Annie probably lying dead.'

'Of course she's not dead. Don't even think about it. She means too much to us all for me to talk like I did if she had a chance of being lost to us and take hold of yourself now for we'll be by the gates in ten seconds and here's Mr Hostler with them open and ready for us.'

The moon was full but the street lights dimmed its glory now and Sam took the car round the island that left us passage through the car park to the great front door. There was a wheel-chair in place and a ramp arranged ready for Sam and Hostler was with us and had my car door open and then Sam's and Sam was in the chair and I wondered how often the hall porter had done this expert work.

Now he had opened the door and was pushing the chair up the ramp and opening the counter that led into the front office.

I could not recognise my own voice as I asked him if it was bad. Bo'sun had told me to take hold of myself but I did no such thing.

'Don't try and hide it from me. Please tell me no matter what's happened. Annie isn't dead is she?'

'Of course she's not dead, Miss. I had a call through from Dr Cunningham and I found out what had happened and rang him back. That's how I had the wheel-chair ready and the gates open. The news is good and Louisa will know it all by now. It was a bit complicated and perhaps and we call it an error of judgement but I don't think any heads will fall.'

# 5

The Head Porter's reception office had the
same plate-glass window that surveyed his
whole world and greeted us with a flow of
warm air that was as comforting as a pair of
open arms. I looked out at the familiar In and
Out signals that kept the consultants as
regimented as traffic lights. It seemed that
they were almost all gone home now. Down
along the wide corridor and placed at
strategic points were the marble busts of past
members of the staff long dead. The
out-patients was closed and the cleaners in,
ladies who worked in pairs with their hair in
neat white turbans who wore spotless white
overalls.

A little nurse had brought us in a tray
covered with a white linen cloth and I saw the
familiar red embroidery of *Wentbridge
Hospital*. It was so familiar . . . white cups,
bowl of granulated sugar, jug of milk. Hostler
had supplied the saccharine in the empty
paste jar. They had forgotten a spoon but
there was a wooden spatula that we could
borrow. It seemed that Hostler was styled for
any emergency. There was the raid siren of

emergency in the air and I knew that it meant an ambulance on its way round the island.

'That's another for Orthopaedic I daresay,' said Hostler. 'I don't have to tell you what the roads are like. You made very good time arriving when you did. I haven't had a chance to get it all sorted out yet but the sister will see you when you've had tea. She told that nurse to send in chocolate biscuits too but catering forgot. It's been a hectic day but when isn't it hectic?'

The small nurse returned at the double with apologies and 'Pussy Galore's' chocolate fingers and Hostler grinned at her and told her the sister had better not hear her. 'Her name is Sister Susan Finegan and if you ever come to be a sister like she is remember to bring chocolate fingers when they're ordered.' Just because the boys like Ian Fleming's books is no reason to call a senior sister out of her name.

Hostler was amused but maybe he remembered the agony about Annie.

'I've had a rush job digging out what happened in Ward Six,' he said. 'There wasn't much time between phone calls and I had to ring back to tell them what I knew and it was little and they were driving Orthopaedics mad right from the first light with people on their way to work and cars skidded into the

112

ditches. Go on above to the new sister on Six. She had this 'comedy of errors'. That's what she calls it but she has it that the responsibility is hers.'

He looked at me and smiled.

'Of course it isn't. It was all that Wendy Nightingale who started dishing out drugs to Annie and then as if that wasn't enough Wendy takes it into her head to ring your Gramp who used to be her doctor and she doesn't realise that he's gone and a new doctor will answer the phone just as he's starting his surgery. Of course the phone was up to its usual tricks. It might have been easier to send pigeons. I had to get on to the hospital to answer the call and get the chair ready for the Bo'sun. I had to make sure that Louisa knew it was not a hanging matter. I hoped that you two would not end in a fen dyke because of this weather. Now I'll put you into Pussy Galore's hands and into her mercies for it's likely that Wendy Nightingale deserved the chop and the sister is merciful if it's passed over.'

I looked out through the plate-glass window and saw an old lady lost. She had been at O.P.D. earlier in the day and now they were all gone. She trailed along the wall like an elderly grey rat seeking the door that would release her to find the bus. There should be a bus pulsating, waiting to take her in and if she could find it it would drop her off at her cottage.

She knew the familiar bus and the man would put her off at her little cottage and Tibbles would be waiting for her on the best chair on the old cushion and the tin of cat food would be for opening and the slaked fire for stirring back to life. The cup of tea and it was home.

'The little nurse thought Annie was dying and no wonder. Don't blame her. She's one of your fen girls. She ran to the man she knew but he was in his grave. She talked to Dr Cunningham but he didn't make sense and the phone was bad. So everybody did the best they could and it was very good. There was telephone conversation between the hospital and Agnes Parva and maybe fears were erased.'

Now Sam and I had been lifted to the floor of Ward Six. Hostler told us we would get V.I.P. treatment and that Pussy Galore was a damn good Sister.

We saw her through the glass door and right enough she was a startling looking girl. She seemed to have everything. She was in a dark-blue uniform and her cap was maybe a model by Hartnell. It was floating perched on her head and a bow under the chin and she

114

was sweetly pretty, her fair hair a platinum blond that swirled tight to her head, not a hair out of place and eyes dark Irish blue, long-lashed. Her smile was soft and gentle as she saw who we were. 'It's Lalage and the Bo'sun isn't it? I'm sorry to have to see you in this kind of situation. It's complicated but things do go wrong. If you could find the time to listen to me you might understand but mine is the responsibility. I should not have allowed it to happen.'

'And Annie?' I said and she told me that Annie was back on the ward after a rough time in X-ray. With luck there was no harm done but there was no result now. We must sit out a verdict. Mrs Tiplady must go through it all again. 'It's my fault not hers. I should have seen it did not happen,' she reported.

It was a funny story if you could see the funny side of it. Poor old Annie had had her barium meal and had come back to the ward and then she had thought the barium meal lay heavily on her stomach.

'I'm sure it did too,' Sister finegan said. 'It's a common complaint and one of our probationers was looking after her. Annie had a bottle of pills in her handbag but it was in the luggage room and she remembered that she had some pills in her bag that her old doctor had given her if she wanted a purgative. She called them 'mouse turds' and indeed it was an apt name.' Again the small smile inviting us to make fun of a thing that might be dangerous. 'Annie prescribed herself three 'mouse pills'. The trouble was with Wendy Nightingale who fetched them from her bag in the store room and administered them to her. She had been accustomed to taking them Annie said and they had never done her 'aught but good.' '

She sighed and went on after a while.

'There is an unwritten law that patients on a barium meal and follow-through never, never, never have any such drug especially if it is not prescribed by qualified people.'

'I should have seen it did not happen. It created great havoc in the X-ray. Annie overreacted and there was chaos. The head man came down and he was overworking on Orthopaedics. He was very displeased and of course Annie was more than displeased. She locked herself in the lavatories for two hours. It took us ages to find out what was wrong but truth will out especially after old Dr Lister's pills.'

She looked at us and I saw the tragedy in her eyes. 'Don't think I'm making light of it. Annie brought it on herself and she is a difficult old lady but it was done in ignorance and that's what I'm here to stop happening. It means that Annie has to repeat what's unpleasant enough but it means we have to wait for the result we should have had in our hands now. We had hoped this result was clear but it was a disaster. I had a talk with her and explained and her only worry was that Wendy would get into trouble. She was right about that for Wendy certainly has got into trouble. It will make her a better nurse and she will never make the same mistake.'

She was praying that the X-ray would turn out normal. It was quite on the cards that there was something in the lower bowel. If that was so Annie had her death sentence but Pussy Galore would never believe it. 'She was such a fine old lady . . . *is* such a fine old lady. She would not admit any trouble in the whole of her life. To her it was the old doctor dying and your parents, Miss Lister . . . then Louisa and her ridiculous baby at her age and poor Bo'sun with 'that dratted disease in his legs' . . . and the baby.' The baby had been a final blow. Annie had asked her what was God thinking of and Pussy Galore smiled again.

'I wasn't able to answer her, Lalage, but I know that there is a lot of prayer going on that repeat X-ray goes through well. It will finish Nightingale if it doesn't for she blames herself for my fault. In Ireland we pray to St Jude the patron saint of hopeless cases . . .

117

'The trouble was that Wendy rang Dr Cunningham in his clinic and it seems that he was up to his neck in some police case. He's taken it very well but it need not have happened. He had a distraught woman in there and a police car, a police woman too . . . one of those nasty allegations that take a doctor's concentration and all sorts of complicated examination. He could have done without an error of prescribing by a probationer. You know I never blame a nurse for a mistake as long as it's her first. We all make mistakes and that's how we learn.

'Nightingale is a good girl and she's tough and self-sufficient like all fen people. Her mother died a while ago and her father married again . . . maybe not wisely. Wendy looked after the house but the stepmother and she did not get on. She took the job in Wentbridge to escape. We'll have to hope she does . . . '

Sister took us in to see Annie who was pretending to be asleep and her cubicle curtains drawn. There was more tea to be drunk and more conversation and it went well. We told Annie that it would soon be over and she might be coming home in two days time and I knew that there was forty hours hard praying in front of us. We told Annie that the barium-follow-through must be done again and she screwed up her face and said it served her right for breaking the rules only she didn't know. Sam had come into the ward for a word and as usual he refused to see Annie downcast and trotted out the old chestnut about the man who died and went to hell. The next day he was walking about hell and he looked up and saw God in Heaven taking His daily constitutional.

'I didn't know, God,' he called up, and God looked down at him, very stern like, and told him that he bloody well knew now.'

Pussy Galore had a hand on the wheelchair in a moment and thought it better if Sam took himself off to the Head Porter's Office, if he thought he was back on his desk but Annie said she was used to wicked ways and let Sam be and she was smiling so he was forgiven but poor Annie worried about the little probationer. It had been a terrible row while it lasted not only from the X-ray chief but from Matron and sister herself.

Wendy Nightingale's eyes were still red and there was talk that she was going to be sent off the ward. Pussy Galore laughed that to scorn and said one should not believe everything you hear in hospitals. You'd never believe it but they said the patients all called *her herself* the Regimental Sergeant Major when she rarely had a cross word for anybody and Sam was flirting with her quite openly and telling her that the whole world as far as Agnes Parva were quite aware that the correct pseudonym was Pussy Galore.

Sister Finegan took it all in her stride and said that was another ridiculous story and the whole atmosphere had lifted.

Sam had it that the cure of constipation was very interesting. We had only to ask Annie and she would verify it that in Church House they had an earth closet years ago. The mouse turds had been modern enough. There had been a time when one doctor had asked his mother-in-law and that of course was Annie, what she had taken for her lazy bowels . . . and she had said she took her knitting.

The whole Jollity Farm that was Church House on occasion moved into Ward Six and finally it seemed that we were thrown out by Pussy Galore and were back in her office.

She got us a glass of sherry and all her carnival was gone.

'Of course Wendy's been reprimanded and that's it. Annie brought it on herself and I think there's no harm done. It was a pity she picked the block busters . . . completely wrong, not indicated at this stage of X-ray. The main thing is to find out what lies in the lower bowel.' Pussy Galore had cat's eyes and she called floors decks and she was hall-marked by the W.R.N.S. The verdict remained and soon we would know. Either there was or there was not and it was her guess that the bowel was normal but that was just an impression. Sometimes she had a power to see into the future. Lots of people think they have it . . . some psychic nonsense. 'There's a feeling about a case and Annie has it with the whole set up of the Lister family at Parva. I attended the funeral you know of the last doctor to represent the Wentbridge nurses. You don't know that and I shouldn't ever have told you. There was this tremendous feeling about that burial so when Annie came in I knew her already. I think I knew she was going to be all right. I should be drummed out of nursing for giving into such thinking . . . forget it. Before you go have a word with Wendy. She misses her mother and she's lonely in hospital . . . and take that charmer off home to Agnes Parva and watch the iced road. We don't want Louisa's child to be without a father through skidding into a dyke with too much sherry on board.'

She let us use her office. Wendy came along presently and of course I remembered her well. I tried to reassure her that the storm had gone by but she had a fixed idea that she might have killed Annie and she was terrified. I made her see that if Annie had malignant disease it was certainly not her fault. She should have known not to use the pills nor yet the telephone for an external call. Personally I didn't blame her for ringing the practice. Wendy was in no trouble and that was a white lie. I thought of what investigations might be to come and wished Annie was home safe in Church House. Then I remembered the day I had tried to buy the toad from Wendy in the pond by the High Street of Agnes.

It was a long time ago and I came on Wendy with a toad in a jamjar and both she and I children.

'We're friends, Wendy, long time. If you want to come to Church House come and see me any time for all the difficult task I had to liberate the toad.'

It was looking down a long lane and I remembered it well. Wendy was going to take the toad home and keep it in the jamjar and forget all about it. I tried to be very persuasive with her, arguing that the toad might have a family. The green was a lovely home and she was depriving it of all that green happiness.

'You were an awfully hard child, Wendy. You took to finance and you drove a hard bargain. You beat me up to 'a little white sixpence' before the toad was mine and that was my money for the week. It was to buy clove bouncers and I went without.'

I laughed at the thought of Wendy with the sixpence held in a tight grip, her hands in her pockets as she grinned up at me and the gap in both our teeth.

'You calculating money-mad nurse,' I said. 'So you've got your come-uppance.'

Sam and I were making our escape and the ambulance was coming round the island with 'another for orthopaedic'. Hostler said goodbye to us and we thanked him. He told us to drive carefully and in these days it was the normal caution on the roads. It was an escape to freedom but not to tranquillity as we passed through the open gates of the hospital and pierced the never-ending stream of traffic under the protection of Hostler's eye. He gave us a smart salute as befitted the ex-service man.

'Take care.'

As we left there was the double-toned siren again as another ambulance rushed its injured to Casualty. Over the noise of the traffic came the banshee wail from further off of yet another on its way in. Accident would be a battle-ground now. It would not ease up till the hard weather broke and spring came and all its flowers and Rupert Brooke maybe walked Grantchester once again but not tonight. It was a hard night in any language.

The fen was in the grip of winter and it had started to snow again with the sky dropping heavy single flakes that threatened more to come. They started the wipers to smear the windscreen and were tiresome and would not yield enough even for a snowman not that we wanted such a toy. In a fen practice a blizzard spelt tragedy and impossible conditions. Civilisation could dwindle and shrink to nothing. The fen people had lived with it a long time. I worried a bit about Louisa's baby. It would be wiser to get her admitted soon but that would start a battle in Church House worse than picking barnacles off rocks. I shied away from the idea, knew that Sam was probably worrying about it and moved my mind back to Six and Annie, wondered if she dreaded the prospect of tomorrow and the preparation for her repeat X-ray. Maybe they would give her a few days rest and I hoped that the Boss man who had been so angry today would forget what chaos she had caused on a day that had had broken bones lining up for his expert opinion. 'Good God!' He might have said. 'The damned councils did not even grit the streets. The whole county was a skating rink and the pensioners must go out to do their meagre shopping. They tell me to keep my costs low.'

Then I was back to the future and my

worries a see-saw. Soon there would be 'the next results', a thought that could not cease to agitate me. Yes or no. 'Either it is or it is not. It will all be well. *The descending colon is normal* or maybe bad news? *There is a cauliflower mass and liver involvement. The prognosis is very poor. The case is inoperable. Mrs Tiplady may have three months to live. She would be a suitable case for the new special hospital for such cases*...Extract from Hospital letter or so I saw it, God help me.

They would be doing the evening round now and settling the ward for the evening . . . see-saw . . . see-saw. It was like a shut-in bee buzzing in my brain and it would not stop. Before the blizzards started again when winter came again Annie would lie in the grave with Grandfather.

There would be another burial. I wondered if the gypsy boy would climb the big tree and listen to the Salvation Army band as it turned the corner into the High Street . . .

'You're whittling Miss Lalage,' Sam said to me. 'And I'm maybe a bit uneasy too but it does no good to worry for worry never does any good and what will be will be. Worry killed the cat. We'll have to borrow the bull terrier from Hostler. She was a great one for killing cats . . . caused no end of worry to Hostler and the neighbours.'

125

He smiled at me and told me I had had a bad time but I must overcome it now.

'The old girl will be as right as ninepence and we'll fetch her out in maybe two or three days and she'll plague the life out of Louisa till she agrees to go into Mill Road. It will be a battle royal. When the wind lies as it lies tonight I've seen the whole of England shut down and drifts as high as the telegraph poles.

'We'll have to watch the forecasts and move if they forecast dangerous snow drifts in East Anglia. There's nothing to beat a north-easter and snow that drifts deep.'

Yes, Sam and I were caught up with 'whittling' as he called it. We had been driving carefully and we were well out of the town now. The traffic had dwindled to nothing but we were coming up to a bend. There was a car that came up behind us and had no time to wait. It went past us when there was no time and then the driver was fool enough to step on his brake. The road had turned to frozen ice and he spun round right in our path, described a full circle, and then started off again at speed and was gone. Sam's naval past was evident in his language but it was caustic with fen salt too.

'Silly young bugger, deserved to be lashed to the grating and flogged. He could have

126

killed himself and us too. Nice thing if the infant phenomenon had to be born with no father.'

Sam had taken to call the baby by this strange name to tease Louisa and it certainly changed our miserable thoughts. I said it was time 'the infant p' was being shifted out to his bed in maternity with his mother. We must see to it. At the moment it would be better if we shifted our thoughts to what had happened in Church House.

'Likely they'll still be dug into the case,' Sam said. 'They were due to arrive as we left . . . Detective Inspector Bullen and a policewoman and that means sex for a start.'

'Does it indeed?' I smiled at him for it was an odd way of putting it.

'Louisa will have to work out how to cope with reception and she usually provides refreshments for the police as well. I hope the 'infant p' doesn't take it into his head to weigh anchor this night of all nights.'

The thought of such a thing unnerved him.

'Rum will do for me,' he said, 'but Bullen always sticks to beer and he never goes over the limit. It's very hard on us all these days with the breathalysers in their own kits. They'll bring Hacker to drive I daresay. Since the day they arrived the master always made the constabulary very welcome. Louisa knows to have beef sandwiches and plenty of mustard. There's ham too. Still there's a chance it will all be over time we're home.'

There had been a big reorganisation in the police in the last years and I have never thought that they approved of it any more than we did. We had got a complete section of men planted into a new area specially landscaped in Agnes Parva. Hacker with the Police dog said it wasn't natural even though Sherlock Holmes his Alsatian appreciated his big wired run. Bullen had been at Harton for years and years where Dr and Mrs Ross practised in a village near Wentbridge.

The police houses were newly erected. The village had it that the paint had not yet had time to dry. Detective Inspector Bob Bullen had charge of it and some of the Harton Police had been moved with him. It was in a cul-de-sac off the Agnes High Street and it was surrounded by a high brick wall that screamed at the thatch of the village houses to keep their distance.

It was like a child's model of a modern Police Station. It was a Noah's Ark without the animals. Each house was the same as the house next door except that Bob Bullen had a double-fronted house as befitting his rank. The gardens were landscaped into equal oblongs for equal flowers and each patch had its clothes dryer and its sand-pit and its climbing frame . . . an adventure playground with a small roundabout that might make the children sick if they stayed on it overlong. At the far end the garage was concrete-floored and asbestos-roofed and the cars were regimented and spotless. The police dog had a special compound and he was snow white . . . an object of pride to Police Dog Handler Hacker. He had a wire run 'did Sherlock Holmes' but the Hackers had a little girl aged four and she had but to cry in the night and he was in the house of the Hackers curled up on her woolly bedside mat on guard. It was completely forbidden and against every rule in the book but Hacker had been born Upware way and had a strict religious education 'five miles from anywhere'. Anybody could tell you soon that all Hacker would say if he was caught breaking rules was 'The lion shall lie down with the lamb . . . don't do neither of 'em any harm . . . and you'll not find kidnappers after my little gel.'

Bob Bullen's house had the office enclosed and that was for business. It was manned at most times and was used for Coroner's inquests and usually there would be some constable at the typewriter doing his reports. They were a friendly helpful lot and they had been adopted by Church House. Tonight Sam knew they were working there and he thought of them now thinking of the Infant Phenomenon and knowing well that Church House was given to putting names on people. Of course it was quite easy to see why the baby of Louisa and himself had got such a title with his multiple sclerosis and Louisa forty-five years of age, it had been a miracle and according to Hacker a 'joyous gift of the Almighty'. It had caused laughter but it was that special laughter that belonged to Church House. The thought of 'the infant p' turned Sam's mind home and he remembered another person with a pseudonym. 'We'll soon be home now,' he said. 'I daresay the Station will be still there for the thatched cottages to swear at. It was just like the planners to plonk it down opposite the basket-maker's cottage and the pond where he grows his withies. Four hundred years it is since those old cottages were built and some of the beams came from the Norman church they destroyed. The world's a queer old place but time will come when the Station is a venerable antique housing estate . . . it's getting on now. I daresay Mother Black will be seen by this not that the paper work'll be done. The Sarge will get Mistress Quickly off home with Jenny Frost.'

'I daresay,' I said, thinking that Mother

Black was another of those pseudonyms that we were addicted to.

My mind was off down the years and I was remarking Grandfather again one more time. I had been home from school for holidays and I had asked him about the hostesses in Shakespeare . . . *Henry the Fifth* or the *Merry Wives of Windsor.*

'Hostesses?' he had said and went to put a log on the fire and then he glanced at Annie who was present.

'Ash wet or ash dry. For the Queen to warm her slippers by,' he said to get time to think.

'Mistress Quickly married Pistol in the finish,' I told him and he said he hoped that they lived happily ever after and Annie told him not to start putting nonsense in my head but he took no notice of her, asked me if I knew Mother Black who lived in the cottages down by the cut. I nodded my head and said that of course I did.

'You might fit her in as a present-day hostess,' he went on. 'She goes to the Duke of Wellington in the High Street and the customers like her. Maybe she gets comfort from the old Duke. She certainly needs it . . . works like a slave that woman. She weighs 'twenty stun' as they say round here. You see her waiting for the lorry that lifts the land-workers at the first light, brings them back to the side of the road at dusk. I've seen her walk the plough in Wellingtons when the beet is being lifted and a stone of gault on each foot dragging her down and she cheerful. Yes, that's the woman for a Mistress Nell Quickly but never believe the gossip in the Duke — Honey. Shakespeare's Mistress Quickly frequented the Boar's Head in Eastcheap in the reign of Elizabeth the First and now we have Elizabeth the Second . . . and gossip is still gossip and don't go in for it, don't listen to it and never repeat it. It can be an evil pastime.'

'They say Mistress Black is no better than she should be,' Sam murmured at my side and we talked about her all the way home and the miles ran quickly too, as quickly as gossip.

We hoped that Bob Bullen would have dealt with the case by now. Of course Mrs Black was mother to Jimmy Black 'the chicken pox boy'. Sam told me that the skipper and by that he meant Jonathan had not half been mad with me about that, about the way I had overruled him. Safe-harmonium indeed! Nice isolation of the infectious disease! Surely Sam and I gossiped enough but it passed the time. Soon we saw the first lights of Agnes Parva and Sam touched the horn. The gates stood open and there seemed to be three or four police cars parked without lights. Then Louisa opened the front door and the hall looked warm and welcoming. The hall lamp silhouetted her and I jumped out of the car to run up the steps to give her an edited edition of the hospital episode. We had already talked to her on the phone from Wentbridge and now I reiterated the tale of the 'mouse pills' and Louisa said that was her mother all over.

'She'll come out of there as quick as she can. She's determined to get home here to bully me to run off to the labour ward if it snows. She'll have me take 'the infant p' wasting his time and my own weeks before the child is due.'

She started and ran back down to Sam who was marooned in the car.

Sam had started on the snow topic too and she said that she had no time for it just now.

'Just wait till you see what we've got up to in the surgery. The Inspector will get Mistress well off with W.P.C. Jenny but Hacker is to take the dog with them as escort. There's a villain loose in the district. He's dangerous and capable of attacking women . . . '

P.C. Hacker appeared to help Sam out of the car and into the wheel-chair. Louisa took charge of the man-handling of the chair up the ramp and through the hall into the cloakroom. I made for the surgery and met Mistress Quickly and Jenny Frost with her and certainly Mistress Quickly was distressed . . . yet not as bad as I had feared she might be. She was wearing what I thought of as her evening finery for her splash at the pub. She had the imitation leopard skin coat but it was old and shabby. The nylon scarf round her head was shedding rollers on the carpet. She was wearing long feather ear-rings in yellow that dangled to her shoulders. She seized my hand in hers and the words spilled out of her and the tears streaked her eye make-up. She had been ill-treated and thumped and her clothes torn off her. Her purse had been snatched and all her money in it. The man had had her carnally in the bottom of a frozen dyke. Dr Cunningham had been obliged to examine her according to the law but he had been kind and gentle. He had told her that no real physical harm had been done. It had shamed her of course and she had had scratches. She had fought for her virtue and bore the marks. The man had had a nylon stocking pulled over his face. There was no recognising him but he was a rough 'un. He had said nothing to her . . . silent as a shadow for all the terror he carried.

Bullen came along the corridor and said the cars were ready and he smiled to see me safe home with Sam. He went out to see Mrs Black into her car with Jenny Frost. It was a tight fit for Mistress Nell and her, was it twenty stun? The springs on her side complained as they took the weight. Then Bullen saw them off at the gate and the police dog handler with them. The Inspector and I went back to Jonathan in the surgery. I recalled him from the days when he was a young Sergeant at Harton but his hair was greying now. Jonathan stood up as we came into the surgery and poured me a dry martini. I perched myself in my favourite position on the counter near where the forms and reports and statements were being sorted. Jonathan was sealing the garments out into plastic bags numbered, labelled and signed. I picked up Mrs Black's panel card and raised my eyebrows for permission to read it. I was free to do so now for it was my job to keep the records straight. Bob Bullen had gone back to his armchair with his tankard of ale on a small table at his side. There were beef sandwiches, ham sandwiches and plenty of mustard.

'It doesn't add up,' Jonathan said. 'She changed her complaint and she acted very strangely. It rings false. First she's in with a tale of having her washing pinched off the line and the next week comes a big police

999 . . . brutal assault and g.b.h. and robbery and her money stolen and cuts and bruises. They could have been self-afflicted but they were minimal. Then she didn't come straight for help. She went off and tidied up for the pub as best she could. She had brought a set of underclothes badly torn but she might have torn them on purpose.

'When they had arrived at the surgery the other clients had emptied out quick enough,' Jonathan said. 'It was like that Thurber alarm . . . THE DAM'S BROKE.' The fen folk are very kind in case of trouble. At one stage she had made a half-accusation. It had puzzled both Bob Bullen and Jonathan.

'It was very dark. I only saw that his clothes were rough and he weren't a big feller. He kinda put me in mind of the daftie gypsy him with the jackdaw that does his talking for him for he's mute and always has been. Then I thought a funny thing tonight. I went to the old doctor's funeral and the daftie was hiding up in the chestnut tree. He liked old Dr Robert for he would see sick animals for him . . . give him capstules and that, sew up a pigeon's crop did it get cut on the wires. I've seen Doctor stop a whole surgery to sew up a pigeon's crop. He had this red thing on his neck at the funeral and it was all wrong but he liked bright colours did the queer fella. I had lost a red drawers off my line a few nights before and I didn't think of it till just now. Sure as anything maybe there's your criminal for you. He wasn't a big chap and that's the sort of thing he might have done and he don't speak neither.'

So Mistress Nell was putting the finger on my Squirrel Nutkin though I had not heard her do it. I hated the thought of how Mistress Nell was surely on a wrong trail. He was a gentle boy and in straight combat she could have made bits of the poor idiot chap.

If that statement got out and gossip started the children would make his life hell. It was hell enough already. He was a kind of outcast. His own people wanted nothing to do with him . . .

We were all three convinced that the boy had never committed such an offence and I thought of the punt that had been iced up in the cut at the back of Church House. It belonged to Squirrel and it was a very precious possession and not in a hundred years could he get it up by himself but I had an idea.

I knew P.C. Tanner was an ex-seaman like Sam and that he came to Agnes Parva with a great reputation. If we got Tanner to lift the punt and maybe brought along the dog handler and his dog and just a small piece of the torn garments, I would come too and we would lift the wreck. The boy would be somewhere about. He would surely come forward to see what we were doing. We must not frighten him ... just softlee ... soft catchee monkey. What I wanted was a negative from the dog. Surely that would let him completely off the hook for he was never on the hook.

I was surprised when the Detective Inspector was enthusiastic about it. It was a simple thing to do and he would pass the word to Tanner and Hacker. Jonathan said that I was excused from surgery and we made many plans for the morrow.

I had rung the hospital late and Annie was having a restless night but was as well as could be expected. She would start down in X-ray at nine in the morning and the best thing I could do would be to ring again after mid-day tomorrow just to see how she was. We could not expect any full results for a day or two. They would tell her that I rang to enquire how she was ...

# 6

It might have been the darkest hour of the night when I woke up and it took me a while to gather my senses and recall what had happened. Inspector Bullen had laid his plans for the lifting of the gypsy boy's punt. It had been submerged and iced up in the cut at the back of Church House. The cut ran from Agnes Parva along to Gibbet Fen where the gypsies had their camp and continued after that on out across the flat land for miles. It had a flood bank and a wash where cattle grazed and I knew every inch of it for aged about ten I had been the proud possessor of a canoe. As Bullen had said last night I must come along with them on the exploration because I was familiar with the terrain. Before he went back to the station he had telephoned P.C. Tanner ex-R.N. and asked him to take charge of the operation.

We wanted to find the gypsy boy so Tanner was to lift the old punt. The boy was a wandering wild one and might not be seen from one month to the next. It was Bullen's guess that he would appear the moment he saw people working at his 'floater'. The

Inspector shoved a package of Mrs Black's torn garments in plastic wrapping into his pocket. P.C. Hacker was to bring the white Alsatian in the dog handler's van. So Tanner would try to lift the old boat and Bullen and Hacker and I would lie low and watch. If I preferred to watch the whole thing I might stay with Tanner and see the Royal Navy at work.

'You want to let the dog see the torn clothes. That's it,' I said and he said, 'Maybe.'

The small bright face of my watch stood at six and I got a panic in the pit of my stomach. Annie would be for the X-ray room today and I knew that she would be frightened and alone . . . praying for mercy and maybe not expecting it. It was a bad time of the day for morale. There were fingers that tapped on the window and I knew it was a sharp frost outside. The branches of the silver birch had been caught and frozen into delicate bones of ice. I switched on the light and got out of bed and the carpet made no sound under my feet. I opened the window and saw there had been no more snow but the frost was cruel. I eased the window shut and pulled the curtains and thought of Annie. I was mad to think that the radiologist would say there was nothing wrong with her. That was a thought of bright day. Now I knew that of course she had a

140

malignant disease. You had only to think of her face and the loss of appetite and all the other cases seen in the practice . . . Boss man in Radiology who had already tangled with Annie would be in no great hurry. In a day or two he would ask one of us to come over. He would put it into kind polite language. At her age this evil thing would be slow-growing. There would be no great loss of life expectation. She might last for months yet but she had a growth . . . a malignant growth in her descending colon. It had already spread to the liver . . . There was no stopping it now . . .

The silver birch tapped its slim branches on the windows and shuddered my spine. It was time I got up and started work . . . made cups of tea and distributed them . . . made a heap of scrambled egg and fried rashers and put on the electric toaster and cut stacks of bread to feed it. The house was warm enough for Sam would have seen to the anthracite stoves, good old Sam! Louisa had refused to let him come out on the cut with us and he was a disappointed child. I knew it. Was *he* not the Bo'sun? He could have told Bob Tanner about the art of seasmanship.

Bullen was to collect me at seven a.m. and he came as the church clock struck the hour and behind him in the police dog van P.C.

Hacker. They were in plain clothes . . . any fen farmers out for a day's shoot. Wellington boots, breeches, old army jackets. Jonathan came down to see us off and told us we were wasting our time.

'That woman is a hysteric. It's my bet she made the whole thing up but she was so definite about the identity. You'll not get an identification out of Sherlock Holmes on those torn clothes if you get an inch of the gypsy. She produced a set of underclothes fit for dusters. I really do not see the point of playing detectives in this sort of weather but at least Constable Tanner will get the old boat up. He'd better have a care. That cut is twenty feet across and it's five feet deep in the middle. Watch out along the bank for it's a skating rink or so I imagine.'

We turned into the lane that ran along to the cut and Bullen looked sideways at me and admired my ski suit. I grinned at him and said I had my double thermal long-johns on too 'as worn on Everest', nothing to beat them unless I decided to go for a swim.

It was not far till we came to the seat of operations and we did not see far in front but we did know that there was something going on. Constable Tanner had stolen a march on us. He must have started hours ago and he had a tractor up on the bank and lights. Of course it was Len Marshall's tractor and Len was in what he called a muck sweat. Bullen asked Tanner what he was playing at but he was pleased with his constable. 'There's initiative for you Hacker.'

'Now to stations.'

They had chipped a deal of the ice away and had a suction pump working to get the water out. Tanner was going very gently with the whole task. It was rotten wood and it would not stand up to much. Bullen said I was to stay on the cut for I knew it like the back of my hand. God knew I had probably fallen in there a dozen times . . . I knew the depth of the water. He went off with Hacker and they sank into the landscape and it was coming light now. He said that the boy liked my grandfather and would never be shy of me. I was to be a decoy. For himself he parked his car down river about a mile and placed Hacker in the other direction with a clear view of the river from under the edge of a long beet clamp. Hacker and the dog were to huddle in under the shelter of the clamp and not to take their eyes off the place where we were at the submerged punt.

'If the boy sees you, Miss Lalage, he'll come to find what's a-doing. Don't frighten him away. I want to get the dog near for just one moment.'

Tanner told me that Mrs Black had let it out after hours in the Duke last night that she had put a finger on the gyppo and I heard again the story of the theft of the red drawers from the clothes line at the time before Grandfather was buried and the fact of Squirrel Nutkin with the red scarf on his neck. Had I not seen it myself? I had not heard her accusation, but she made it strongly to Bullen and Jonathan and now apparently in the Duke to send it on its rounds. Bullen could not ignore it but he was suspicious of her now. It did not sound likely. It was a popular crime in Agnes. The boys were sanded with the usual trouble-makers but the gypsy lad was a loner. He might get 'some aggro' if Mistress Black made her accusation public in the pub. 'The silly moo' as Tanner said.

I kept a keen look-out up and down the cut but I could not see Bullen anywhere nor Hacker. They had vanished into thin air. I searched for Squirrel Nutkin as if I was doing a jig-saw puzzle looked for a part of the picture that was spread before me. I thought of the hunched shoulder and the dragging leg . . . the low squat size of him and the restlessness. The shabby coat with the poacher's pocket where he kept the jackdaw.

I listened for the now familiar cry but the

tractor was noise now and there was nothing else to hear. We were after a creature of the wilds. I knew it. Tanner had lent me his jacket to sit on and I had found myself a seat in an angle of a fallen elm and very comfortable. There was a north-east wind blowing with a shrill high voice. They said in the village that the north-easter would 'thrap you'. I wondered how he kept still. Maybe he was away on one of his travels. He was certainly nowhere near the cut. He had no cover for the snow was just a-dusting. Then I saw him and I had to look and look again. Down river thirty yards there was a fallen poplar that had made a natural bridge. Another tree had come down to lie at an angle covering it. The boy lay as still as a stone pressed into the angle and he was camouflaged in his rough tweed jacket. His hair was nondescript and uneven and thinning. His hands were purple with the cold and in ravelling mittens. He had a tattered scarf but no collar. I saw the big safety pin that held his shirt closed.

'There he is,' I said softly and jumped to my feet.

'Jaaack,' I shouted. 'Is it too cold for Jaaack today? Come and see what we're doing. We're lifting your punt with a tractor and it's going to be O.K. or we so think. Come and see what we've done.'

He came running down the bank towards us and he was excited. He was almost with us and then he turned and ran away again and his left leg dragged behind him. The jackdaw followed him flying above his head and I thought we were going to lose him.

Len Marshall cut the tractor engine and cupped his mouth in his hands, 'blared like a bull', as he might have said himself. 'See the way we got the ice off and the craft swaddled like a babe agen' hurt. Cor! That'll sail a treat come the fine weather.'

The boy had crossed back over the fallen poplar to the other side and had crept along the bank to come opposite where we were. He bent forwards and peered over to where we stood and he took in the swathed hull and the safe passage through the ice. He looked at the cables that were going to provide the power to do the pulling up the bank. His face grimaced like a small monkey's might have done showing the uneven teeth. He nodded his head and did a little dance up and down of pleasure and excitement. Then he was back along to our side of the cut having made no trouble of the bridge.

'Take no notice of him,' muttered Tanner. 'I'm seeing I've got all the ice out of the way. I'm going to pull her up by the bow and God be with the sailors this day. We'll have to take her an inch at a time. Her timbers must be rotting. It would take just one wrong move to break her up into splintered wood.'

He passed the time by telling us how he had such a craft as a child on the Broads and his father a deep sea fisherman. There had been a flood tide one spring and a freak north-easter and his ship had ended in a pile of broken planks at Bacton Gap. He had never got over it. It made him realise what ship-wreck could be. I thought he was joking and then I realised he was deadly serious. He was telling Len Marshall how he intended to take the ship up and the boy had seen they were oblivious to him or seemed so. He was in his own way absorbed in the careful wrapping of the hulk with the fresh canvas webbing and the ice clear . . . and a path cleared in the water. He was excited to see the tractor begin the pull and the way it moved an inch at a time. There was a slant to the bank but no hurry in the world . . .

'My old woman knows how important this is,' said Len. 'She was a fisherman's daughter down at Yarmouth . . . real Yarmouth bloater . . . We'll take the lad back to the Home stores. He's an old customer and no price and no money necessary.'

So the tractor juddered and inch by inch it won against the lift of the bank and the boy was darting up and down watching every gain we made. The bow was lifting clear of the water. I sat on the fallen elm and was glad of Tanner's coat. The day was bitterly cold. We were almost clear of the ice now and the bow of the punt was showing. An inch at a time up she came and the jackdaw knew there was something joyous. 'Jaaack. Jaaack.' Squirrel Nutkin too was pleased with what was happening. I knew about what life can do by this. At any moment there would be a cracking of the old timber and we would have the loose plank floating in the cut again drifting down the cut to rot to become wood to salvage for winter fires. I could not bear it. I think P.C. Tanner felt the same and so did Marshall. Squirrel Nutkin seemed not to feel the north-easter even in scarecrow's clothes. Now and again he came to where I was and jumped up and down with his joy and I knew he had little joy in his life. He moved restlessly in the same strange way a marionette might move on strings but no puppet would wear such dilapidated garments. His shirt was torn and it had no collar just a khaki scarf, ex-army. Still he reminded me of a squirrel as he had that day at the church. Always the old dragging of his left leg tormented me. Once he crossed the cut again to watch progress from the far bank and from a new angle I saw the lobsided shoulder and the swollen cheek bone . . . the result of a blow no doubt. He clapped his hands again and nodded at us across the cut and smiled again with the uneven teeth . . . and ran back to us again. It was our policy to be totally unenquiring to him. It was all taking a long time. I was not surprised to see Inspector Bullen come strolling along the bank a long way away. The jackdaw was safe in the poacher's pocket in an instant and the boy hared back to where the boat was being drawn up . . . not much farther now. He looked towards Bullen and searched my face and I smiled at him, said O.K., and gave him a thumb's up sign and thought I was like a mother that put a dummy in a child's mouth. I was filled with guilt that such a creature as this should live in Agnes Parva and I not make it my business to see that such ones were not neglected. Annie saw to him sometimes and he knew she would have food for him if he came to the back door but I left him alone. The gypsies out at Gibbet Fen were an unsavoury lot and they had cast him off to sleep in a tarred wood shack. I had gone there before now and he had shown me a pigeon that I knew Gramp had stitched when it tore its crop on the electric wire. Gramp had sent the boy into hospital to see what could be done years ago but there was nothing. He was 'ineducable', he was wild. He would not be shut up. I wondered uneasily now if it was hopeless. His was a birth injury they said and he had irreversible brain damage. It was best to leave him free . . .

They were turning the floater over on its face and the last of the water was running out in small dribbles and the time ran slowly.

It was ten minutes later that Hacker appeared out of nowhere with the white Alsatian and stood looking down the bank to where we stood. The jackdaw took itself into the poacher's pocket and from there it protested but a ragged mitt covered it for comfort. Hacker strolled along beside the dog and Hacker walked along beside him and kept him on the leash. The boy stooped down as if to hide and I imagined that there was a silence over the whole fen. Then the gypsy stood as straight as he was able to and reached up for the sky. The low clouds were flying fast and the wind had turned even more bitter. Squirrel Nutkin was like himself as I saw him . . . a squirrel standing on his hind feet and one arm held high as if he wanted to pick something from the heavens. He made a clenched fist and I asked myself what he was about. His hand came slowly down in an arc back to earth clenched still and he smelled at the air seeming to search a scent as an animal might. I can no more describe the whistle and we have talked about it. We all heard it but we have never heard anything like it before or since. His clenched fist was held out towards the dog. There was no doubt he called him and the animal was down on his belly and trying to crawl towards him. It was impossible that Sherlock Holmes was trying to escape but he was. I heard Bullen shout 'Let off the leash' and knew that the dog was glad to go. It was all wrong. I was close enough to the gypsy to see him watch the dog race to him. The fist was still clenched but it opened to the animal as if there was something the Alsatian recognised. It went down in front of the lad and crawled along to his feet and he bent to fondle its ears and made much of it, almost gathered it into his arms.

The dog rested his head on the boy's shoulders and adored him. It is the only word I can use. Then there was this same whistle and the sky seemed filled with it so shrill that it was like a high cold blast from the North Pole. The boy was sorry to send the dog away but he pointed it back the way it had come and it obeyed him. It ran straight and fast along the line to P.C. Hacker and at his feet it lay down nose between paws. That was all. We saw it but we never understood it. There are more things in heaven and earth as Bullen said. We never had an explanation of it and the police dog never acted strangely afterwards but I am leaving out the important bit which I put in now. The Inspector crossed the space to come to the van and here he produced a handful of coloured rags. Sherlock Holmes never moved his head. He never even looked at the rags nor sniffed at them.

He sighed and dropped his nose between his paws again and went to sleep and Bullen said it was fair enough. 'Test negative.' Bullen said. 'That let's the boy out.' I could still see the way the dog had stood and looked up at the boy. I do not think I will ever forget it. I will never forget how the whistle sounded either for there is no sound like it heard by human ears. Squirrel Nutkin could pick sounds out of the sky. Maybe you could explain it by saying that the boy had a way with dogs but we had never seen such a way before. We were all a little quiet for a while and then we busied ourselves about the punt.

The work was done now and the craft was on high land but there was more to it.

'Poor little bugger,' Len Marshall said. 'The weather man says there's hard weather to come and heavy snow. I have a big barn up at mine and I reckon we'd better put that floater under proper cover. Do I fetch the trailer? We could run it home in no time and the boy could see where it goes and watch over it, know it's O.K. That's a wild one, true romany that little old boy. You'd not know what he could do did you see into his mind.' The boy rode with the punt on the trailer and was seen by Agnes Parva to be accompanying the police and the gossips went a little further and maybe the trouble went a little further. Mistress Quickly had pointed the finger the night before. It was P.W. Jenny Frost who surprised us all. She had come on duty again and only now had she heard of the statement made by Mrs Black. Somehow she had missed hearing it the night before. It had been made confidentially to Dr Cunningham and the Inspector because she 'had been ashamed to tell the Policewoman' P.W. Jenny knew as well as I knew that Squirrel Nutkin had had a red rag on his neck on the day of my grandfather's funeral. Nobody knew but the thief that Mistress Quickly was given to having her drawers stolen off the clothes line. A few days before the funeral such a thing had happened and then she said she had seen the same garment on the boy's neck as he hid in the chestnut tree and that was a lie.

Nobody but the policewoman knew that it was she who was responsible for the whole dreadful accusation. She had gone to the funeral to represent the police and she had in her pocket an old silk handkerchief. She knew he liked bright things and his neck was chafed raw. I had not been there when Mistress Quickly made the charge. Anyway I could not have identified the silk handkerchief.

'So the gossip can be halted here,' Inspector Bullen said. 'I'll have a word with Mistress Quickly and get a confession out of her on what we have now. I'll bet the whole story is false from start to finish. The dog gave us a negative out on the bank today. Now P.W. Frost gives us a red silk handkerchief as a clue that cannot be denied and I have it in mind that it's time that we keep an eye on that boy. We have a few 'yobboes' in Agnes who could make that lad's life hell. He can probably whistle the birds out of the trees.'

★ ★ ★

It was after surgery that Jonathan heard about the episode of Sherlock Holmes and Bullen's decision to see that the 'yobboes' did not molest poor Squirrel Nutkin. He made me describe again how the lad had reached up to

154

the sky and plucked down the magic that carried a trained police dog to his feet.

'The dog didn't want to leave him,' I said. 'It would never have left him. We're all convinced of it and poor Hacker is upset about it.'

Jonathan poured out a generous Martini for me and reached for the bottle of Glen Livet. He poured out a good dram and toasted me across the desk.

'So we have a raggedy boy who can fist magic out of the sky?' he smiled. 'If you're not telling me fairy stories I don't think that the chap needs much protection from Bullen's 'yobboes'. Quite possibly he could look after himself.'

# 7

Jonathan had kept in communication with the hospital about Annie's progress. Unfortunately one of her plates had been mislaid and it had to be found. It had just vanished and the Boss-man was pulling the X-ray staff about its own ears. That was Jonathan's description as we relaxed over our drinks. Poor old Annie had had to hang round the clinic far too long and she was apprehensive and tired. In the afternoon before I got back the missing plate had turned up but there was more scrutiny to be done on it. I had intended to take the Humber into Wentbridge for a visit to Six but Sister Pussy Galore had phoned the surgery and advised me to ring her. It was the easiest thing for her to bring the trolley complete with the phone to Annie's bed. It would stop the patient 'whittling' if I spoke to her. The result was not through yet so she could give me no final result. It looked good but better be sure than sorry. They were very pressed for beds and completely crowded. They had beds up along the main corridor. *It was a red alert.*

'Sister will ring you and put Annie on. That

will be she I think. She's always on time.'

I was startled but it was a wrong number and a flood of apologies. I set back the phone on the bracket and tried to relax. Almost at once the bell ran again and I got a mental picture of Sister and Ward Six, the telephone trolley and Annie in the bed with the curtains drawn for privacy.

'Sister Six on the line with Annie to speak to you, Miss Lister. She's had a long day but she's behaved very well. She's our prize patient today so I'm putting her on to you now. We can hear the church clock strike this minute at Agnes. Can't we Annie?'

'Ain't that like a miracle?' Annie said and I thought her voice was old and very tired . . . thought that the news as I feared was not going to be good.

'I thought I was never going to hear your voice, Miss . . . never hear you again and now there you are and the old clock striking too. That were a rare treat and Sister's been so kind to me. She had them send me up a lovely special tea, aromatic China blend and petit fours . . . like we used to read about in Cranford. She's a real angel we have on Six.'

Annie was making the best of it but she was very low. 'I'm not going home like they said. That's bad but it's not my real worry. The bad thing is Louisa and the news that she has to go into Maternity in a day or so for an X-ray. They want to have the Infant P in that awful machine to have his picture taken. It's not natural nor yet right. It's a way to find out when he's due to be born.'

Annie had actually 'called the dear baby out of its name' herself. It was strictly forbidden and she had not even noticed it. Now she changed the topic quickly and said that they had lost one of her reports and that was what the delay was. She had been listening to the ward T.V. too and the weatherman said that there was a big fall of snow to come. She knew he was broadcasting from London and she didn't believe a word he said. If she was ever up in London she couldn't see the sky from start to finish. In 1947 it had been lost like the man said and he was right there. The whole of the country was blotted out. She could remember it . . . weeks and weeks . . . no electric, gas or nothing.

She was worrying about it because if she soon did not get home she might have to stay on in hospital and then what would she do? I heard Sister's laugh across the line.

'We usually make the patients wash the dishes and polish the coal, Annie. It's not too hard when you get used to it. She's fine now Miss Lister. Laughing her head off . . . actually laughing. What did you say to her?'

'Just get her to tell you about the infant P. That's all, but don't do it till I'm off the line. Then ask her to tell you about old Nurse Pepper.'

'What's about the Infant P and who's Nurse Pepper for God's sake? You don't mean our old Nurse Pepper?'

Annie was on again in a shot for she had heard me mention Nurse Pepper and she filled it in for me.

'Sister will know about the old nuss . . . never ever one like her. She wouldn't have X-rayed a babby just to find out when it were due. Did she put a hand on the mother's belly Nurse Pepper. She'd tell you when it were due. Not only that, but she was near enough right if it were a boy or a little old girl. You could buy the right-coloured wool and know the weight to a few ounces. The weight of the baby, not the wool! Louisa is a nuss herself. She should know what date she's due. She put it there herself . . . the no-good girl. X-ray indeed! I'll give her X-ray if she ever dare appear in my sight any more.'

'I'm sorry Annie. I'll have to cut in on you. I have a call waiting. There's a poor man 'whittling' to know if his wife's had a boy or a girl and we can't find Nurse Pepper.'

Looking back on the conversation now I am almost certain that Pussy Galore worded her conversation another way. She said that the man wanted to know if he was to be a father or a mother, but Annie knew it was something very urgent.

'Goodnight Annie, sleep well. I'll give Nurse Pepper your regards next time I meet her in Parva on her old iron horse. Come home as soon as you can. The house is lonely for the sight of you. We'll come in and fetch you as soon as we get the word.'

★ ★ ★

I laid the phone on the rest and sat against the edge of the counter. In no time at all, Louisa and Jonathan joined me.

'No result yet, Lalage?'

I shook my head, told them that there was an important piece of jig-saw missing.

I had told Annie that her daughter was due for a film of the pelvis in Mill Road at any time and Louisa was scornful.

'You know there's too much fuss about the infant P,' Louisa said scornfully. 'I've thought for a while I mixed up my dates. The head's not gone into the pelvis yet . . . not engaged. Great Bed-Pans! That don't happen till the thirty-seventh week. Then I'll have a shelf on

160

the front of my belly that I can set a cup of tea on . . . and I'll have frequency from pressure on the bladder. You're all medical people. You know it. I'm lost in my sums. I'm going to cut my appointment for a week or two. We'll have to see what becomes of Annie. I'm not going to spend my last three weeks waiting for the Infant P to take it into his head to descend to his proper station in life.'

I had been frazzled with worry for days and I had fretted that the Infant P was hanging fire. I watched Louisa with a sharp eye and she never had the slightest interest in spending a penny, so that sign was negative. I even paid some attention to see if I could see any sign of a shelf in her tummy . . . result nil. Jonathan packed me off to bed early. He gave me a white tablet to take to ensure a sound sleep and I slipped it into my dressing gown pocket and thought I would have it with my mug of hot chocolate. I had a good look at Louisa's shelf area as we said goodnight and then I was between the warm blankets.

It was my own fault that I had the strange dream. I had involved myself with Mistress Quickly and her story as interpreted by Gramp. A day or two before that night, I had gone into the library and found a red leather-bound copy of *Henry the Fifth* by

161

William Shakespeare. I had actually discovered the Boar's Head Inn in Eastcheap. The chocolate had been too hot and I had burnt my mouth with it, so I had set it on the bedside table to cool and had gone to sleep.

I was in my study at school I thought and for some reason I must have got the red copy of *Henry the Fifth.* It was later in the night when it fell off the bed to the floor and I woke up with the fright it gave me, or did I wake? I thought I was at the Boar's Head Tavern and that we were all off to France to Agincourt. Sir John Falstaff was dying and Mistress Quickly was nursing him. Grandfather had told me that there was no better description of a dying man.

I was back at school yet we were all off for the battle of Agincourt. I recalled it through the night hours till the fall of the book startled me to half-wake and I found the cup of drink cold and rippled across the top. Mistress Quickly was dressed in a wimple headdress . . . I remembered what she had said but she was gone.

'I put my hand into the bed and felt his feet and they were cold as any stone. I bade them lay more clothes on his feet. I felt his knees and then upwards and all as cold as any stone . . . ' Grandfather closed Sir John's eyes with his hand and bound up the dropped jaw with his red silk handkerchief . . . told me to remember the coldness of death. I was bathed in the sweat of a nightmare and I knew I must try to pull out of it. In the bathroom I threw cold water on my face, went back to bed and into the horror again. Mistress Quickly told me that she had sinned, but that she had fear of Pistol who was her husband now. He was going to fight at Agincourt and might be killed, but she didn't care much. He was a soldier and must expect it. The trouble was that he couldn't leave the sack alone, not that she didn't drink too, but she worked hard for her money out on the fen fields in the winter. Maybe she *had* supped the rent money but he had had his share of it in the old Duke in Agnes Parva. It didn't make much difference. The rent money was gone and she had said it was stolen. She had said she had been robbed and that she had been ill-treated which she never. She'd accused the gypsy boy, said that he was the one who stole her things off the line, which he never. Her husband would have his belt off at her. It was all a lie and mixed up into stirabout. Annie came into it and she knew Annie was for death . . . the cold stone. It went on till I found the white tablet still in my pocket and I drank it down with cold chocolate and fell into a deep pool of sleep . . . black, deep, dreamless. Somebody opened my door during the night and pulled the curtain to. The telephone rang and I half heard it. The bell was ringing for church so it must be eleven and morning. It was likely eleven and Sunday. There was the sound of tyres on the drive and a deal of talking and laughing from downstairs, but still it passed me by.

Somebody had come to sit on the side of my bed and Jonathan had pulled back the curtains on a snow blizzard.

'Try to get with it but take it easy for a start, Honey. There's been news but it's all good. Annie's come home by ambulance with a clean bill of health. She has put her clean apron on and is busy making hot scones for the ambulance men . . . nothing wrong with her and that's official.' I was still dreaming . . . or was I?

Quick scones for the ambulance, that was Annie right enough. I pushed my feet into my green slippers and pulled on the green velvet dressing-gown. I told Jonathan that I did not believe a word he said and then I ran like a rabbit for the kitchen. There was a battle royal between Louisa on one side and the ambulance and Annie on the other. They had been told to collect Louisa for Mill Road for admission and there was an argument about 'the shelf' again. Jonathan said he agreed that

164

she might be only thirty-seven weeks, but there were other causes for a non-engaged head. Then Annie saw me and came to take me in her arms and she had grown smaller and more frail. We ate buttered scones and the butter ran down both our faces and the tears too and Annie complained to me about that no-good daughter Louisa, who had all her things tidy and neat and packed in the suitcase to go. The ambulance men said that if she had any sense she'd take the lift to Mill Road. It had rained on the heavy snow and the road was as bad as it could be. It would be anybody's guess if they ever got to Wentbridge. At that, Annie said it was unsafe and she locked Louisa in the Frazers' bedroom and Sam raised his eyes to the kitchen ceiling and asked God to deliver him from women and their affairs.

Louisa would be in Mill Road in a day or two anyway and Annie must be worried no more. There was a Sunday dinner to cook and it was to be roast beef and Yorkshire pudding and she was hungry for the first time in weeks. She beat up the eggs for the batter briskly and the fat sizzled and spluttered. The ambulance men moved off on the gravelled drive and skidded into the road and when it was past recall, Louisa appeared downstairs again and was received with forgiveness. The village of Agnes Parva settled down to its usual Sunday afternoon stupor. There was a miasma of gossip just beginning to rise about the affair of my Squirrel Nutkin. The tongues had been wagging in the old Duke, even in the short time that had passed. He had been seen with the police, when they had lifted the boat and that started it. There was talk of the red at his neck at the old doctor's funeral. The corner boys began to chivvy him, screamed him away from the chippy and all he had was the aroma in the air to fill his empty stomach. A flint hefted by a lout hit him above the ear. He shambled out of reach but the blood stayed as witness and Bullen found it, near a doorstep and his later mind marked it down as more trouble. The boy seemed to have disappeared with the coming of the blizzard. The snow was deep enough now and it was still blowing hard. Presumably the boy had some secret hide of his own, but a worry niggled the Inspector's mind that would not let him rest. He sent Hacker out with the Police dog, but there was no sign of the boy. He might have disappeared into thin air and his people out on Gibbet Fen had no knowledge of his whereabouts nor did they care much either.

'Daresay he'll have gone to his uncle out

Peterboro' way. That one is a wild bird that flies where he pleases . . . likely he's snowed up in some hole or corner and when the spring comes, he'll come out again for the warm. He 'ont come to harm . . . never has done. His sort is God-protected.'

As for me, I was shaving away the snow with the special instrument we used for such activity. It was a large wooden scraper with a long handle. It could well have been used as a sweeper in a boat. Like the revelation to St Paul on the road to Damascus, my dream of the night before recurred to me.

Mrs Brown alias Mistress Quickly, the mother of Billy of the chicken-pox had spent her rent money and that meant trouble. She had thought out a way to avoid her husband's taking off his belt at her. Or had she? She had thought out a plot, a false accusation. She had acted out a pantomine, carried out her plan. The gypsy boy was her target . . . easy enough. He had no tongue for denial. I wonder if my dream was a solution of the case. There was a deal of thinking to do. Maybe it would be wise to set my idea in the lap of Inspector Bullen. I found the *Henry the Fifth* where it had fallen by my bed and sat with it by the window, looking out at the steady fall of the snow. I thought of Mistress Quickly in her wimple and the story she had spun for me. It was possible. More than that, it was probable. I thought for a long time and the darkness thickened round me. I thought for a very long time.

# 8

Inevitably the cold weather brought its toll of illness among the elderly patients and the wild creatures were hard hit too. No matter how often we fed the birds, there were pathetic casualties in the garden and along the hedges. The frost still held but the snow eased up. Louisa was treating her coming baby as a great joke saying the weather was far too cold for a sensible baby to come out especially if he has as much sense as his grandmother. He would stay in the warm where he was. Annie said it was fool-talk and Louisa should think shame of herself for behaving like a skittish girl at her time of life. Louisa was laughing and joking far more than usual, but I knew she had fear. There was a way she took to looking at Sam an odd time, as if she were storing up the memory of him because soon she might not see him any more . . . the way she was silent sometimes, a deep sadness in her eyes . . . the way she had taken to looking at Annie, putting her arms about her, kissing her . . . a little girl running to her mother for comfort.

Annie was as grumpy as ever and mighty

169

sharp with those who reminded her that she had been ill and must take care of herself. Sam was his old cheerful self, working harder than ever, assembling the machine parts, pretending that he was not out of his mind about the thought of Louisa and the baby.

There had been a conspiracy in Church House for some time before this that I did not understand at first. It started with Annie presenting me with a lovely length of white Irish tweed, though where she got it I have never discovered to this day. She wanted to take my measurements for a suit of homespun!

She picked an old orchard moss green velvet collar, the very shade of the colour of the roof of Agnes Parva church.

I had much gratitude in my heart and stood for the fittings with patience. Louisa and Annie were planning to regenerate me into an attractive young lady, whom a man might want to marry. They had taken to match-making and it was Jonathan they had in mind, so first I had this elegant suit that might have come from the Rue de la Paix. Then my little black suit was trimmed with a strip of shining black fur. Louisa had grinned about that, declared that she had found it dead on the fen.

I found I had money now that I worked as

practice receptionist. I expected Annie to counsel me to save it. I was taken into Wentbridge by Louisa when she went into Mill Road for her ante-natal examination. There were sales on and nothing would satisfy Louisa till we had 'done the shops'. Louisa was an expert on remnants and she picked out some for us both. She also advised me to buy a pair of shoes. Louisa said the doctors had advised her to rest. Nothing would please her more than to help Annie with the dressmaking. The layette had been ready for months and now Louisa had taken a craze for glamour. She wanted to see what she could do with her face, if you please. I went along with the cult to humour her, so we experimented for hours in her bedroom with face cream and what Annie called stick-lips. In fact Annie came to the conclusion that we were like a pair of kept women. At any rate we all laughed a lot and one evening, Jonathan took us both over to the surgery sink and scrubbed our faces for us.

For all that Louisa declared that the Expectant Mum must keep attention 'centred upwards' to the face, there was no doubt that it was *my* face she worked on. At one stage Sam must have been roped in to help in the combined operation. He passed out sugared statements to me. I had a restful quality that he admired when I sat with my feet primly together and my hands quiet in my lap. It was a good thing that I had passed the tomboy stage, when I sprawled on the hearth-rug at his feet. 'Oh Sam!' I said reproachfully for I knew he was having me on, but he took no notice of my sarcasm. To carry the campaign further, my most disreputable shirts and pants mysteriously disappeared one day after the gypsies had been, for all that nobody ever discovered what had happened to them. So perforce, maybe I took more interest in my behaviour and sat at the place that was mine at the counter at surgeries in a crisp white coat, with the dark-red 'stick-lip' that Louisa had chosen for me carmining my lips, wondering what I was trying to do. I had no plans to fall in love with Jonathan. I was interested in his happiness and hoped that he would find it with Fenella if he really was in love with her. I was full of doubt both about his and my own feelings. He was very casual about her. I thought I existed in his mind as some kind of a pleasant sister.

I dragged her into conversations and praised her . . . said she had lovely eyes, but he turned his head and grinned at me. 'Your own eyes are far more lovely. Haven't you noticed? She hasn't those sweeping brushes you use for lashes, or if she has, she bought them in pairs at the chemist's.'

He was very candid about her and told me about her. I knew it already . . . about Fenella being a cousin, child of his uncle who had the works where Sam's stuff came from . . . how Fenella had wanted him to go for a Harley Street existence.

'He wanted to buy Harley Street and me for her. She had always got what she wanted. She's not lovable really, just acquisitive. She must have more than the other little girl . . . never thinks much of anybody but herself.'

We had gone skating one day on the lonely miles of the frozen washes of the river and the snow was going to spoil the skating, for it was too heavy and it was drifting. We had stopped, breathless by a clump of willows and he stood and looked at me and his eyes were warm, because he liked me.

'Give me a person who knows what it is to be without. A plant that endures the drought puts down roots. Your Grandpa would have told you the same thing, keen gardener that he was.'

He steadied himself by holding to the willow branches and I skated circles about him and hoped that he noticed the new stretch nylon pants and the scarlet sweater.

He did not even look at me and I thought of Fenella.

'Do you see that black fen gate a mile away? I'll give you two minutes start and beat you to it. If you win, I'll toast the muffins and get my face scorched at tea . . . '

He laughed and I asked him what if he lost?

'Then I'll carry your skates all the way home.'

Bitter-sweet memories, I knew now how easy it was to fall in love, but I knew he was not the one for me. I sped away from him across the washes and was glad I could skate well. The wind whipped past my hot face and I listened to the ring of steel against ice. He cheated of course for he started off at my heels and caught up with me, flew along at my side, turned his head to watch me, so that I lost my fine free style and was hopelessly out-matched. Then he knelt at my feet and took my boots off, tied them together and looped them round his neck.

I have been playing with time, as if I played with the hands of the old clock in the hall, for Annie had come home safe and sound and the wind had turned bitter and chill, straight from the east. This was the last of the skating for the snow would surely come now, as it was forecast. There were black clouds

174

building up on the horizon and it had started already, as if it looked down out of the swollen darkness. There was a scurry of wind and handsful of flung feathers. The wind was rising to shrill through the trees along the drive. The cloud bank had built up and up. It was pleasant to let ourselves into the hall and walk along to the comfort of the sitting-room. He toasted muffins and buttered them and indeed, it was a bitter-sweet evening for me, for I knew now that I loved him and would never love anybody else, yet it was his happiness that mattered. I would have to see Fenella and plead his love for her, tell her what a man he was. She would be staying in Wentbridge in a week or two — in the university centre. I would make it my business to go and see her, even picked the white tweed to wear with an orchard moss green velvet collar, the very shade of the colour of the roof of Agnes Parva church.

We changed at last and went along to surgery and a few of the hardier spirits turned up to collect their prescriptions. For the most part we sat and talked gossip. He was worrying about a patient who was due for her baby far off out on Black Horse Fen. If the snow went on, that whole fen would drift with this blizzard. The farm house might be cut off. We all thought of poor Louisa and 'her shelf'. There were thirty miles of drifting snow at a guess between us and Wentbridge now, or would be by morning and this was the road with the dyke at each side of it. Oh, God!

We went to bed early and I fell asleep with the whine of the blizzard in my ears. I woke to the start of the telephone bell in the hall. It was four o'clock when I snapped on the light. Jonathan came tapping softly at my door.

'That's Sister Fleet ringing from Black Horse Fen Farm. She's been out there with Mrs Smith for three hours. She's afraid the road will drift over. There's no shelter there . . . always drifts.'

He was going out at once to see that all was well. He'd bring her back if the baby was born. He was going to telephone Will Papworth to put chains on the tyres.

Will was not hopeful . . . said it drifted six foot at Black Horse Fen 'times it snew. Always did when the wind lay in this direction.'

I was out of bed and thankful again for the remnant of green velvet and the little gold buttons. I had made coffee, hot and strong. There was no chance of me being allowed to come too. Will explained that it would be a matter of digging the car out every halfmile. I packed the kit . . . all the black cases, that belonged to home midwifery. Nurse Pepper might have made it on her 'iron horse' in the days that were gone. 'The old doctor would have told you how it were, Miss Lalage. I've dug him out a score of nights same as this.'

I wandered uneasily about the house when they had gone. Will Papworth had been well equipped with spades. He did not think they would make the house, but Sister Fleet was there and no doubt the baby too.

'Cor! I hope Old Mother Smith has the son this time. If he has another little old gel, don't know what he'll do with five to find husbands for.'

The sound of the phone bell woke me from a half-drowsy state and it was the nurse.

'He'll not get through,' she said when I told her Jonathan was on his way. 'The baby's here and Smith has his son at last. I'll hole up here, got my sleeping bag . . . wait till they get a snow-plough out. Tell Doctor nothing to worry about and nought to do . . . Lalage, listen while I can keep the line. The wires are coming down all over. I think we're going to be cut . . . '

There was a click and a burr and dead silence.

It was still dark in the night outside the window, when I heard the Daimler return. It came round the back to the kitchen door. The storm had risen in the last hour and I was dressed and waiting. I raced down the stairs to get the door open and I might have admitted two snow men, who seemed to bring a blizzard with them. I pulled them into shelter and knocked too much snow all round the floor of the hall. Jonathan grabbed Will Papworth by the arm and took him through to the cloakroom and said Annie might be more pleased if they left the mess in there. I told them quickly that I had heard from Sister Fleet out on the farm and that the baby had been safely delivered. Then I ran along to the kitchen and was surprised when the lights went on. There had been a candle left burning on the table in case.

'Mrs Smith had a son,' I said as soon as they followed me in. 'Sister has a sleeping bag and she'll be asleep by this. She said she'll stay on the case till the snow-plough remembers her . . . case all tidied up. Nurse Pepper will stand in here. It's all arranged as usual.'

Jonathan was delighted that Smith had done the miracle . . . had produced the son after five daughters. Will Papworth grinned and said that Dibber Smith would be out of his mind with the boy. 'He'll spoil the lad rotten. I can see the little old gels taking turns to push the pram.'

I asked Will why he had not taken off his coat, but he said he would be away again directly. They were sending out a helicopter to drop fodder on the washes. He had to see that the men knew what they were doing, not that they would attempt it now with the way the storm had blown up. Still he had to be on hand. 'Cor! I'll miss Church House breakfast and now I mustn't stand here gabbing all night. I must be on my way smartish.'

Jonathan was thanking him for his help, but he waved gratitude aside and was gone. His own car was waiting in the barn and I knew that Sam had been in the Admiral Benbow since very early, seeing to the stoves and the many chores. Louisa was not down yet. Annie was supposed to be resting, but I knew she would appear at any moment. There was never any chance of keeping Annie resting, especially when there was something doing and news on the way.

Jonathan was grey with fatigue. I set about clearing up the hall a bit and then started the breakfast and sure enough Annie came creeping downstairs in her spotless white apron and replaced me by the stove. Her ears were wide open for the news of the Fen Farm baby and she was delighted that Dibber Smith has his son. The kettle was beginning to sing on the stove.

'Is Louisa not down yet ... lying late today? The rashers and eggs and the fried bread will rouse her, when she smells them. I have some fresh scones in the oven too and make plenty of toast child. There's new season's marmalade.'

I told her that Will Papworth had been and gone again. They had been planning to bring fodder for the cattle on the washes. She shook her head at the helicopter.

'They'll not manage it in this blizzard ... no lazy man's farming today.'

I knew that Jonathan was worrying about Louisa. It was impossible to make the trip to Mill Road. The road was always drifted in this sort of storm. The water in the dykes by the roads was a constant hazard, never far from one's mind. Nurse Pepper has fixed to stand in, I thought to myself, asked myself what was keeping Louisa and then nearly jumped out of my wits.

There was a sharp knock on the back door and it opened on Detective Inspector Bullen, heeling wellingtons off on the step, shrugging clear his great coat and putting it in the cloakroom. In the kitchen he arrived wearing a white polo sweater high about his ears.

'I'm sorry to intrude but I'm on the lookout for Will Papworth. I believe he was out with the doctor last night to Mrs Smith of

180

Fen Farm. I want to contact Will on urgent business.'

'Will's been and gone again,' I said. 'He's hoping to drop fodder to the beasts on the washes, but he's not much chance to do it with the latest tornado.'

'So there'll be no helicopter today,' the Inspector said. 'It's a pity, but it was a poor chance anyway. It's a non-starter.'

The Detective Inspector was very willing to draw up to the table and Annie saw to it that he was provided with a fine breakfast. Annie passed out the plates and by this Sam had come in and asked us all where Louisa was, but we were all assured that she had slept it in and the rest would be good for her. Bullen had been tucked in to a place beside me if ever I managed to sit down. Just now I was helping Annie with passing out the usual breakfast in emergencies and the aroma must be invading the whole house. Bullen was confidential with me. He wanted the helicopter particularly to see if it could spot the gypsy boy out on the fen . . . his body most like.

I had heard the rumour and I heard it again now, very silently and confidentially.

'Maybe I told you myself, Miss Lister. I can't recall it. There's a hue and cry out for the gypsy lad. We found human blood on a

181

doorstep in the High Street and he's not been about. Looking for him is like looking for a needle in a haystack. It's hopeless with drifting.'

Bullen was enjoying the comfort of the kitchen and he knew I was to be trusted. He lowered his voice when he spoke to me. It was a rich secret for me only.

'Mistress Quickly is out of her mind. She came to see me and said it was all her fault. Nice time she thinks to tell it. Now she has it that it wasn't the gypsy lad . . . don't believe it ever was. She wants to confess to me. Agnes Parva is driving me off my nut.'

I could understand his anguish. The boy was often missing, but now there had been blood on a doorstep. They had had it reported and had done very little and it might seem they were negligent . . .

There was a silence while we all dug into our breakfasts. Sam worried about Louisa. She should be down by now.

'Just give the smell of the breakfast a bit more time, Sam. She'll be down,' Annie reassured him. 'I'd best see where she's got to,' Sam smiled, and took his way upstairs.

There was a rich secret and Bullen couldn't resist a whisper in my ear, mostly repetition in his eagerness.

'Nice time Mistress Quickly thought to

spill a confession to me personally. So it wasn't the gypsy lad? I never thought it likely. Now she must clear her soul . . . tell me of all people and I'm the law, God have mercy on me! I'll have to mount a search.'

We had almost finished breakfast when Sam came in and told us that Louisa was on her way down and that she was shipshape, though the blizzard was worse than ever.

'It's going to be the same as '47,' Annie declared. 'The County Council won't salt the roads far less dig us out. The council men will keep a few lesser villages in touch, but they still won't have heard of snow ploughs. It makes one able to look after oneself. I never miss the electric. It strains a person's eyes. We have the Willingham Church lamps shining and polished after all the years. Vicar let us have them as a gift at the time. The Master never would have them converted to electricity. They burn oil still and I'd thank you, Sam, if you set them in the surgery for tonight's session.'

Bullen had cornered me again and reminded that I had been born in Parva. Had I any idea where to search for Squirrel Nutkin?

I said that, to my mind, I imagined he would not go far from Len Marshall's barn where the punt was sheltered. I said I knew the cut like the palm of my hands and it had been my playground most of childhood. I could skate and I could ski.

There were all kinds of hidey holes and 'Nutkin' could choose any one of them and lie hidden. I said it might be an idea to take Hacker and the police dog. The dog had liked the boy and he might fetch him out. I was very confidential with the detective, but I knew the cruel ferocity of the fens. I knew myself guilty of not being kinder to the outcast. It was wicked that a whole village could neglect one small ill-wished child. It was easy to say he was born free and to ditch my responsibilities. *Mea culpa! Mea culpa! Mea culpa!*

'I'll help you, Inspector. I'd like to sit down and open my mind to the task, try to remember the places I played long ago. If I emptied my mind, the answer might come. The question is where does Squirrel go when the storms rush the skies and blot out his kingdom . . . '

He thanked me and told me that he would bear me in mind.

Then the door opened and Louisa came in and I thought she had a pride about her. I noticed that she was in a fresh uniform and her gold fob watch was swinging on her breast. Annie was impatient with her and told her that the baby on the fen was born for hours now and that Farmer Smith had his son at last.

'Five little girls and at last the son,' Louisa laughed. 'I'm so happy for her. Maybe it's a good thing to have a baby, when the heavens are dead set against it.'

Louisa laughed and said it was time we were all getting used to the idea that she might be going to have a child. She had been in labour since the small hours but there had been no point in alarming the whole household. They were sharpish contractions now, but nothing to be alarmed about. Sam sent his knife and fork flying off the table and Louisa went over and set him fresh silver, placed her hand on his shoulder in that way she had and she said she had no idea of going anywhere . . . no place to go and she happier where she was. Annie was frightened. I knew by her. She told us that last time, we had been cut off for ten days and it was a long time to let a dear little babby wait to be born.

Bullen made an effort to get out of the room, for it was no business of men, but Annie pushed him back in his seat by my side and cupped her hand round her ear.

'Did my Louisa say the Infant Phenomenon were on its way?' she asked.

'How's it going Sister?' Jonathan asked her

185

and Louisa said it was 'nothing to fright' anybody. 'It's fine, just what I thought it would be. I'm not going anywhere and there's anyhow, nowhere to go. This is what I always wanted . . . never thought I'd have the good luck.'

Jonathan's hand dug into my shoulder and he smiled at me and said he imagined Church House had known babies born down the years and this cheered Annie mightily. The old doctor had often taken command and always it had been a happy day or night, when a baby came.

'We have a new commander now,' Annie said, 'One to give orders. It will be the first child to be born in this house in his time, but we'll get through as we always did. There have been so many babies in the years that are gone, and each is the best yet and always with that great happiness in the bearing.'

We stood there in a kind of tableau and the discussion was soon started and finished.

It was time that Louisa finished her breakfast and then set about putting the infant's clothes to air by the kitchen fire on the horse. I was to brave the elements and go to the Post Office stores.

Sam was to take over the surgery and see to what visits were in, that must be done. The main thing was to see to getting the telephone

186

fixed. It was a doctor's phone and had priority. I must tell the Post Office lady she should get it working without delay. I had to scavenge the Post Office Stores. Always in this sort of time, salt and oil and candles went under the counter . . . never a candle to hand. I must not stand any refusal from Mrs Northrop, Postmistress . . . Jonathan asked Bullen to come with him. Nurse Fleet's cottage must be broken and entered. He wanted to borrow any items of kit he could find . . . the gas-air apparatus and cylinders for oxygen, for the emergencies of midder. There was a list of stuff to check to fetch from the chemist's. Louisa was helping me get kitted out for my walk to the Post Office Stores. I was wearing the pants and sweater I had used for skating before the snow ruined the ice. Louisa had lent me her old navy mack and my school scarf was wound round my neck. It was worse than I expected when I stepped out through the back door. The snow was blotting out the future to a dark grey. Horizontally the wind was whipping powdery cloud like spindrift round my feet, like the waves of a stormy sea. Above everything and through everything was a shrill scream. It tore at my garments . . . Ned Pearson skidded to a halt in his Range Rover and moved into the shelter of the Admiral Benbow Inn, as I

187

closed the door behind me.

'I'm leaving the Range Rover for young Cunningham. Your Grandfather always had it if he wanted it in this sort of weather. Nothing to touch it, your Grandfather said. I'm going to put it in the barn now and young Cunningham's free to use it when he likes . . .'

'I know it will take most of the drifts,' I said, but the wind tore my words away and Ned was stowing the Rover in safety.

He made his way along the High Street and disappeared and I thought what good neighbours we had . . . I bent my head and followed him along the way. A few of the hardy householders were out with spades.

'Mind you don't get yourself blow'd away, Miss Lalage. That's six-coat weather today.'

'This is treacherous land, Miss. Don't force your way out in it, where no mercy is. The tempest don't know where its strength lies on a day like this . . . seen the cattle strewn across the reaches of the wash.'

I made a rush for the Post Office door and the bell tinkled in welcome. Mrs Northrop was standing behind the counter in her white apron and I knew that her arthritis was 'playing her cruel.' She had not closed an eye all night. She hadn't recognised me at first sight . . . I looked like a walking snowman.

'This weather is like to lie the same for weeks. It ain't come so hard since the big fall, when fifty of Will Papworth's beasts were drowned in the floods after.'

Mrs Northrop was like Mrs Noah in her spotless apron and she told me that her leg was like a rat eating her with the screws and if I had come to ask about the dratted phone, there was no phone in the whole benighted area, nor hope of one.

'But Louisa's baby's on the way,' I exclaimed. 'We can't get her moved to Mill Road, the way it is now.'

'But the whole of England is blanketed,' she objected with delight in the disaster. 'Every road is blocked this minute. It's an easterly airstream too and you know what that means. The cars are stranded along the main roads. Ain't no chance to go nowhere.

'Poor Mrs Frazer,' she said. 'Wouldn't you feel sorry for her? I expect you're after candles and oil and salt. They ain't sanded the streets as usual and the poor old folk are coming down like ninepins.'

Poor Mrs Northrop was generosity itself once I told the news to her. Her cellars were open to me. Nothing was impossible. I was packed with all kinds of contraband and departed laden down.

'Mrs Frazer was elderly to start a child and

with himself the way he was and the Bo'sun one of the war's heroes, but when the war is won, there are plenty that forget what you've done . . . Look at yourself and your whole family lost . . . and that don't butter no parsnips for you . . . not but what the people of Agnes worship the ground you walk on.'

It was time I got home and the weather was the same as it had been. I felt melancholy and imagined I had the black dog on my shoulder. Opposite Nurse Pepper's cottage, I saw Pepper herself trying to load her Mini. It was far too much for her. The blizzard was almost lifting her off her feet. I shouted out to her to wait till I came back with a car. I conceived the idea of borrowing the Range Rover. It was a long time till I got home and dumped the shopping in the porch. Then I opened up the gates of the Admiral Benbow.

Why should I not borrow Ned Pearson's Range Rover for Sister Pepper?

I went out of our gates far too fast and only skidded twice. I arrived at the nurse's in a very short time.

It was strange how quickly time started to go. I was exalted suddenly. I had grown up. I could drive a big powerful car. I threw in the kit and helped Sister Pepper in beside me and she was kind enough to have more faith in me than I had in myself. I made it safely and loaded the nurse to Annie and then Sam took the car from me and put it in the Admiral Benbow . . . told me never, never, never to drive the Range Rover again. I might have killed myself and worse still I might have killed old Pepper.

I found Sister Pepper in the kitchen getting on with the routine work and she thanked me warmly for the help. I was astonished at the versatility and power of the Range Rover . . . decided that I might use it one more time and then smiled at Sister and said maybe not.

The blizzard had dropped quite suddenly and it was as well. Annie was tearing a strip off me for taking the big car.

'You came up that High Street at 70 miles an hour, Lalage.'

The argument died down. Sister Pepper was one of the family and Louisa thanked me for risking my life for the child. I knew Sister Pepper so well. I remembered how she was Gramp's nurse and how she used to make me butter-scotch at Christmas and birthdays. Her hair was as white as snow and she wore the uniform of the District Nurse, in navy blue, and the plain round cap.

'I should not have taken you in the car. I wasn't good enough for you,' I said and she said, 'Hush child. Don't you think I know what sort of girl you are . . . take more than an oversized car to fright you.'

'It didn't fright me,' I lied.

Louisa's bedroom was changed. It had been prepared to be a lying-in room and I felt uneasy about it. You would never recognise it from the pleasant bed that Louisa shared with Sam. There was a table of instruments now and a bath under the bed with a rubber sheet that dipped into it. The washing-up basin was laid out and the doctor's towel and a new cake of soap. There was a medical smell and a large bottle of Dettol. I asked Louisa how she was and she told me that she had no complaints. The time dripped away and nothing seemed to happen. Louisa took time off to relax and take deep breaths with her contractions. We sat down to lunch and it was a good one. We all assembled for it, but nobody seemed to eat anything. I wondered how long it would be. Would it be born at all? Jonathan was sticking close to the house and the contractions were stronger. I saw Jonathan examine Louisa's tummy, noticed that he smiled and that he said Louisa could have her pethidine now. I watched the shiny point of the needle, but for all the fuss she did not make, Louisa might have had nothing.

Nobody told me a thing. I guessed it all wrong and I suffered an agony of pain on behalf of Louisa. She made no complaint

. . . slept now and again and Sam came to see her once and he suffered so much that he was not invited any more. He sat in the Admiral Benbow and tried to work and everything he did went wrong. Then he came into the house and hid himself in the old nursery nearby and waited.

'I don't really want the gas-air, Sister. It's not bad enough yet.'

Sister Pepper found Jonathan in the kitchen talking to Annie.

'If you'd like to get washed up, Doctor. It's time.'

Jonathan was in the bathroom and scrubbing his hands with the nail brush. Pepper made a great business of taping up his gown and his mask and snapping on his gloves. Louisa was on her left side and her face deep in the pillow and she had the anaesthetic mask in her hand. I saw Jonathan's eyes watching me over the mask and thought how people's eyes were flattered by a mask.

'It's nearly over, Louisa. You've done very well. If you want Sam's hand in yours, now's the time . . . only to say it. He's suffering more than you and he's hiding in the nursery and maybe in need of you.'

She just nodded her head.

'Yes, oh, yes . . . I thought I could do

193

without him, but maybe it's not so easy. I'm a bit lonely for him.'

He came clumsily enough into the room and tried to be not in the way. Sister Pepper tucked him out of the way, saw him comfortable by Louisa's shoulder, his head down to whisper to her. I saw the tears on his cheek and knew they were no business of mine. It was all going to happen and it was going well. The head was appearing at the vulva and the hair was a black line that flowed down wetly.

'The head is here to stay,' Sister Pepper remarked. 'Strange the way they put it.'

Jonathan had a grip on what he called the presenting part. He could control the delivery of the head and he knew what he was doing. Of them all, I may have been the only one that had no idea of procedure. 'Hold my hand, Lalage. Don't ever let my hand go.'

I put my hand down in the pillow beside her, shut my eyes tight and bit my lip through. The head should be easing out, but I did not want to look. There was a splash like a salmon as the waters went and at once a child that cried.

'La! La! La! La! La! La!'

'There's your son safe and sound, Sam. You've got a fine boy.'

There was all the business of childbirth,

but I kept my head away and could not bear to look at Sam nor yet at Louisa. I knew that Jonathan watched me closely and I wondered why I could not appear to behave as a sophisticated young lady. There was so much to be done and Sister Pepper and Jonathan were getting on with the conduction of modern midwifery in a home delivery. I wanted to cry with joy and never leave off. The bath was prepared and Pepper was seeing to the bathing of a brand-new baby. Annie would be waiting. I imagined how lonely it would be in the kitchen.

I was ashamed of the tears on my face, as I put the question to Jonathan.

'May I ask Annie to come to see him?'

He grinned at me over the mask and he was very relieved that it was all safely over.

'I think you'll not find Annie far away. It's fitting that she should be fetched here at once. I'll take it as a favour.'

Presently we all watched the ritual of the new baby's bath and it was a ritual as old as time. It is no good trying to describe the happiness that seemed to have come to stay.

Sam managed to dry his tears, though I had seen them, but then he likely had seen mine. There was happiness and to spare. I thought we would all be happy for ever after, but maybe I was wrong about that. I thought that the world was a wonderful place.

At any rate we all got used to this small individual, who inhabited Louisa's room and who spoke with a brand-new voice.

Annie was inclined to take charge of him and that was because she knew Sister Pepper trusted her. We all walked in fear of taking any attention of 'Himself' when he cried, but slowly we all settled down and the house was a happy laughing place, till I remembered that I had a task to do for Detective Inspector Bullen and I had forgotten all about it.

Then about a week after little Sam's birth, I cleared my mind of everything else and remembered my childhood and the fen as it had been. Back I thought and back to the childhood days, and I remember how it had all been at the beginning of my time.

# 9

The death of the gypsy boy was to be news in the days after the birth of Sam's son. He was four days old when the reporter and his camera man skidded into the ditch on the outskirts of Agnes Parva. They left the van where it was, to be picked up later on, took their equipment and set up their headquarters in the Duke of Wellington, started their work. There was a boy missing and not to be found. A missing child in such weather was good for a story and this boy was a strange little character, mentally backward, dumb from birth. There seemed to be no chance to get a picture of him but the regulars filled them in so generously that they had a roseate idea by the time they finished of a wild type of gypsy boy, who was a cross between a raven and a squirrel and lived in a nest in a tree.

There was a gibbet, that had been shifted to a place beside the cut too where it would be out of the way, and a great oak tree, which was possibly the biggest and oldest in East Anglia. It was beside a mere called 'the ballast hole', but to all accounts, this was an evil

197

spot, full of old junk and bicycle frames. It was grown over with nettles and brambles and thorns and every kind of rubbish . . . a place of ill repute. There was 'a haunt' on the mere. Mrs Northrop from the Post Office had it. It was a sad history from more years than anybody could recall of a crazy woman who drowned her baby in the mere, returned and drowned herself in a tempest of tears. She had been seen as 'a haunt' by many of the villagers, always at the full of the moon, standing in the water of the ballast hole, her greying hair invested with water. The whole area got an evil name. The parish council wanted to shift the gibbet out of sight and they put it up stream beside the dead oak, where it was out of the way. The whole area was desolate. Children played there no longer. Over the years, it turned into a waste land and at last it was closed off by 'barb wire'. It was no good trying to take a picture. Besides there was nothing to see in this snowfall. The whole area had drifted deep . . .

In a day or two, there was an evening edition of the *Wentbridge News* and the missing boy took pride on the front page. There was a line of police probing the cut with long poles, feeling for a body and finding nothing. There was a statement from Mrs

Northrop and a horrible description of the 'haunt' and the terror she had caused in the whole village. The newspaper article reminded me of James John Bryan, now my solicitor, but always my friend. His mother had died when he was five and he had come to live with my grandfather and as a companion for me. My parents were dead and I suppose he was kind of surrogate brother, but it was a very happy arrangement. I remembered the old days and how for three years we had played in the big old oak tree house 'as lone survivors'. It was many years ago now, but I could recall the way the old craftsman, Jordan Ison, had put a spiral staircase in it. I wondered if the tree had any of its fittings still surviving. I must speak to James John and ask him if he had seen the newspaper. Also my conscience pricked me about Inspector Bullen. I had promised to help him find the gypsy boy. I went into the nursery and remembered it vividly. There was a great deal of old 'treasure'. James John and I had shared a desk and he had kept diaries. I looked them out now and glanced through them. Jordan Ison's spiral staircase had been the glory of our lives. He was also responsible for the witches' windowpane in the bookcase and for the antique tea caddies, where we kept secret letters. The rocking horse was just as lively as ever. I remember the way Fenella had admired him. 'Children,' she said . . . The old tree house was like a sleeping beauty now, I thought, enclosed by brambles and wire, desolate, deserted and dead.

Had it lain thus for a hundred years?

That evening, after the surgery, I put on my snow boots and walked along the High Street to Len Marshall's shop. There were some messages to fetch for Annie and I wanted a breath of the too-fresh air. The light shone out to welcome me and I remembered that the black-out was a thing of the past. There was a child with his nose pressed against the window, but I could not see who he was. He was wearing a coon-skin cap with a long tail down his neck, so that made him 'the chickenpox kid'. I thought it polite to pull the tail of the cap gently and say 'How!' and then Len's bell rang as I went in by the door. The signs of the war being a thing of the past were there. The biscuit tins with the glass lids were on top of the counter after a great many years . . . not too many assortments yet but they would come again. It was a comfortable, roomy warm shop and it had a tortoise stove like the Admiral Benbow Inn, with a dark green painted bench where the old men could sit and talk, and smoke their baccy.

'I see you're entertaining Davy Crockett, King of the Wild Frontier,' I laughed at them. 'The man himself,' growled Len. 'He's got a little old sled on a bit of rope. I daresay he's after stores for that magic log cabin of his.'

I shoved over Annie's shopping list and then asked Len if he had any sugarstick hidden away anywhere, for I thought Jimmy might dislocate his nose against the plate-glass window from the pangs of hunger. There was a big drawer below the biscuits and it was only a moment's work to transfer three pink and white sugarsticks to my pocket.

'Gee! Thanks Len. I'll bring him in while you get the messages and let him have a warm at the fire . . . '

'It's a secret where they came from, Miss Lister. I'd have every kid in the school down if they knew I was a philanthropist . . . '

Jimmy had been well content to start off on the first sugarstick. The delicious minty smell gave the shop a wonderful old-fashioned aroma and the talk was all about the new baby and the Bo'sun. I wanted to go to the barn and look at the punt that Len had stored there and I was welcome. I knew how to open the door and how to turn on the light. The old floater was drying out a treat. Jimmy accompanied me and I passed the other peppermints over.

'Gee! Ta ever so, but don't tell the other kids. They'd stampede poor old Marshall.'

I collected the groceries at last and thanked Len and said goodbye, went off along the dirt path to the barn, with Jimmy Black trotting along in my footsteps, and I stopped to give him another sugarstick. His eyes shone as he thanked me and opened back the paper without delay.

'I know what you're about, Miss . . . same as them all. You're helping to find the looney. You know he's hid out and you think he's maybe done for by now, but he ain't. That blood weren't nothing. It were only a box fight. One of the big lads tapped someone's nose and it wouldn't lay off spoutin'. He had that sort of konk. It's stopped now.'

I advised him to lay information to the Mounties.

'I might if I meet old Bullen.'

But he said that he knew where the looney was and now he said it again.

'I do know where the looney is, honest Injun, but it's a secret, cross my heart and hope to die. You'd have to swear. Anyway all the kids know or most of them. We bring him beans and that. You know, provisions. The Mounties think he's dead. He ain't dead.'

'I wouldn't betray a secret, Jimmy. Is he safe?'

'He's O.K. He's got a kind of haunt. She'd be spooky, but she'd not hurt you. She stands in the water and blubs all the time, but she's been drowned for hundreds of years.'

I remembered the desolate place that had run to waste land. I had not been near it for a very long time, recalled skating on the mere when I was very small. I remembered the big oak tree where I had shared the tree house with James John. Then they moved the old gibbet to that part of the mere and it all became a dump. In my day, I too had been afraid of the haunt. The whole area had the name of the evil eye. The village people gave it a wide berth. From a long time ago I remembered James John saying that the treehouse was full of owls. He swore that he had heard bittern there and he was not going any more and I had been sorry. It was a lost sad memory.

Jimmy had opened out the last sweet paper hopefully and I saw he was ready for another.

'And that's the last, so it's got to be made to last. This is all true, I suppose? You're not making it up?'

'It's God's truth, but you're not to go anywhere near that old tree . . . not safe for people like you and it's a dirty rubbishy rubbish tip now and the haunt might get you. I must go home now, Miss. I'm late and my mother will murder me. I'll have to run as fast as I can and keep the secret for me for the kids would punch me if they knew I let it out and thanks for the sweets . . . thanks a lot. Mind how you go now.'

He turned and pelted off as fast as he could go and I watched him as far as the barn. I knew he would be back before long for he had left the sledge behind and by now I knew that it was being used to carry rabbit skins and maybe a few dead rats as well.

'I knew you'd be back,' I grinned at him. 'I was minding the furs for you. Good season's trapping.'

I went home along the High Street past the police houses and tapped at the Inspector's door. He was sitting in front of the fire and well I knew it was my duty to tell him what Jimmy Black had told me but I waited till I had time to think it all out. If it were true, he was presumably safe enough. It might be better to have a look round and I had promised Inspector Bullen to do this and then I had been caught up in the new baby to the exclusion of police matters. I offered to borrow the police dog . . . take him for a walk, in places I thought likely for hides. The boy would never desert Len's barn, I said. He would want to watch the 'floater'. It was my guess he was hiding out in a square central enough in Agnes Parva. There was a map on the wall and I traced out an area. I picked Len's barn and took a mile about it. I included the cut where the police and Len Marshall had lifted the frozen-in 'floater' and towed it up to the barn. Then I followed the cut on till it came up behind Church House and out to the desolate area, that I thought of as the place of the sleeping beauty. It was waste land now and useless, but behind the barbed wire was the dead oak. It was impossible to get to it, but one could try. On along the cut again and back up to the barn again. It was all drifted snow and very rough land.

'I would be very glad to take Sherlock Holmes out for a walk one day. There were as many hidey holes along the bank of the cut. That dog would nose the boy out, no matter how much snow he had for a hide.'

Bullen was not all that enthusiastic about the idea, but he laughed at my civic spirit. We fixed it up that I'd pick a Sunday unless the weather got worse and then I made my excuses to say I must get home now. I had had a busy day and I had not talked to little Sam yet. He must be tucked in for the night. Annie scolded me for staying out so late and I said I had been talking to Jimmy Black, but I kept the secret safe, though I was bursting to tell it and see what they all thought. I went to bed at last and read some of the diaries from the nursery, remembered what a good companionship I had had with James John. I tried to redraw the tree house in my mind. It had been the dream of any child and I could remember the way Grandfather and Jordan Ison had taken the winding staircase from a row of demolished cottages . . . I should have married James John, but it all ran away from me. My parents were dead and Lucy had said yes first time. I thought it would not be happy and there was rumour in the village that it was not, but then Agnes was always full of false rumour. Now I was in the middle of trying to get Jonathan back safely with Fenella, yet full of doubts that it was a good idea. I wondered why I could not mind my own business for once. I knew very well that I had fallen in love with Jonathan . . . or did I? If I had another chance to marry James John, I would not take it. I loved my childhood friend as if he were my brother. I had such ecstasy for the touch of Jonathan's hand on mine that I felt faint with wanting him.

'Maybe he loves you . . . maybe he don't, maybe he'll marry you, maybe he won't . . . maybe he would if he could but he can't' said the Bo'sun, too often just to tease. I went to sleep at last and knew I had the folly of all girls in love and the next day I was assisting surgery and finding it hard to keep my mind on my work. I had a letter delivered by hand from the solicitor's office asking me to call to see J.J. on business and I worried a bit in case we were not managing to hold on financially.

He laughed at my worried face and told me not to fret.

'You've done very well, Princess. I suppose I might say it's the opposite, but I've got a secret.'

'I got a secret last night,' I said glumly. 'It hasn't brought me any great joy.'

His secretary brought in two cups of black coffee and some chocolate fingers and asked me how was the baby and I filled her in on the bulletin. She was kind enough to give me a small knitted coat on behalf of little Sam and took herself back to her office.

It was very quiet for a while. James John had a Dickensian room with deed boxes on shelves and a glorious coal and log fire, but he had gone to look out through the window. His voice was low.

'I am totally ashamed of myself. It all came of a letter, which was Father's, being directed to my desk, opened before I saw it was his and having opened it, I read it and went on reading it. It's the devil.'

He looked round at me ruefully over his shoulder and his face was the face of his former self aged about eight years.

'It's been the hell of a job putting it together again, so that I could return it to Sheila's in-tray 'virgo intacta'. My secret is worth hearing, Princess, but I must not tell it to you. I wouldn't do it, if you weren't making a bloody fool of yourself. It comes of giving fathers and sons the same Christian names or more or less . . . damn nuisance all my life.'

He came round to frown at himself in the mirror over the fireplace and then turned round to frown down at me.

'You're doing your best to marry off Cunningham to his ex-fiancée. Look here, I'm sorry for all this. You'll almost certainly kick me out and never speak to me again, but the poor fool is just as much in love with you as I was. Who wouldn't be? It shows that you love him. They all know it. I can't let it go wrong this time. You're the one he loves and given time, he'll ask you, but not this minute. He doesn't want to be a fortune-hunter. It's all poppycock, but you are a lady of substance now. That new stockbroker I got you did wonders for you, but he's not a rich man . . . or was not any such thing. He doesn't know what I know and I'm not telling you. Don't listen to me. That uncle of his that gives the work to the Bo'sun has been observant of Cunningham and his way of work. He's made him a deed of gift . . . a substantial deed of gift and that's all I'll say. So Jonathan Cunningham will have a letter from Father in a day or two wanting him here. There will be a few days of dilly-dallying. There will be a transfer of capital and John will take you in his arms and ask you to marry him . . . do you the honour. Oh! for God's sake will you stop trying to push him into Fenella's arms? Just cancel all ideas of it. They don't want each other.'

My brain could not work it out. I knew it was true suddenly and remembered things he had said that fitted in. My fingers touched the pack of the nursery diaries that I had brought for J.J. I had intended to show them to him and tell him about 'Coon-skin-cap' but I changed my mind. I would make my provisional investigation with the dog on a chain . . . one Sunday . . . next Sunday, if it snowed no more.

'I thank you . . . don't know how to do it . . . know you think it not honourable, but it was. You were always the chap in silver armour, J.J. Thank you for being James John all those years ago.'

The tears were filling my eyes and running down my face and I ran. Sheila at her desk wondered what was wrong with me and I left little Sam's present behind. It was like Jimmy's sledge. Sheila brought it over to Church House herself and left it for Louisa. I went walking across the land on the way to the cut, on till I came within view of the big oak in the distance. There were telegraph poles down and they were propped higgledy-piggledy. The waste land was empty and deserted. It started to snow again and put down a curtain between me and the great oak. It was all blotted out as if it had never been. My thoughts were mixed in my head. I was late for lunch and I had forgotten that it was ante-natal day. Jon ran a tight schedule. Louisa would have covered up for me as the clock struck two, though she had not started back to work yet. Annie had no time to scold me as I ran past her. I was through the kitchen and along to the surgery. My face was scarlet as I displaced Louisa at her desk, just admitting the first patient, and I sent her back to little Sam.

'I had to see James John and he kept me late, I'm sorry.'

I gasped as I recalled the present from the secretary for Louisa for it still lay on James John's desk, or so I thought.

'Do you think we could get started if you're ready now?'

Jon's right eyebrow came up as it always did when he was angry. Abjectly I apologised, said it was unforgivable of me and it would never happen again. The clinic was busy. It ran right on till the surgery was late in starting too.

For all that, the dinner was splendid and we were very tired but in top form. I had not stopped wondering when the doctor would receive his delayed letter from J.J.'s father . . . Lawyers were never too swift in their communications. It seemed that the phones were never going to ring again in the fens. It was almost like Cranford. People had taken to dropping in little notes by hand. After days, I began to think I had dreamt the whole thing. How could Jon have thought I was too well off to propose marriage to me? I still considered I was more as less as poor as a church mouse, but I had had a great stroke of luck in the stockbroker that J.J. had picked for 'my portfolio'. I did not know at this moment what he was talking about, but money was easier, James John told me. I watched the letter box and the third day I saw John Bryan Senior's clerk slip in a long envelope. Annie opened the door and took it in personally. She found Jon and delivered it and he left it unread on his surgery desk. We were no wiser, till he told us that John Bryan wanted to see him personally and would be very suited if he could call at the office about 10.30 the following day. There was a deal of business for discussion, but it was nothing to worry about.

From then on, the tension started to rise. There was an electric current that ran through Church House from attic to cellars.

Annie put on the black coat she used for festivals in church and delivered an envelope sealed with his seal ring and the hot wax he used for medicine bottles. The hat had a feather that could only belong to a 'lady of the manor'. I drove the Humber and watched her leave the letter in the clerk's hand. Then we drove home across the street. I did not worry about her catching cold. I knew she had two thermolactic vests on.

They were all talking behind my back. I had only to walk into the room for silence to fall. Jonathan had read something important. He was making up his mind to propose marriage to me. It was all true but he was going to be sensible about it.

'Marry in haste and repent at leisure' the Bo'sun hissed in my ear and I had to grin at him. 'So it's at last, but I'll have to have it signed with that lovely red sealing wax for I didn't really believe it true.'

The appointment went on for two hours between Jon and J.J.'s pater. Jon came home as happy as ever I had seen him, but he told us nothing. He started to try to engage me in conversation, said he wanted to ask me something and then cried off. It ended quite suddenly at last. He took my shoulders between his hands and spoke to me in a low voice.

'Do you remember the day I first met you? You fell off the ladder and I hadn't a chance of catching you. Anyway you laughed and said it was your way of coming down a ladder. I fell in love with you though I didn't know that was what it was. I just thought this was the most lovely old house I had ever seen. It had an atmosphere of happiness about it. I had been here a very short time, when I traced the happiness to yourself. You had a kingdom of your own and you were concerned for mankind . . . totally concerned. You *were* this house, but I knew I must not aspire to marry you. My prospects were dicey and might be for some time, but we've done well between us all. That uncle of mine took a fancy to you the day you met and advised that I ask you to wed me. I thought you liked me. Oh God! This is a very peculiar story. One should not be so prosaic.

I should tell you that I adore you and I will never marry anybody else. My uncle told me that I would never meet another girl like you. I know money isn't of the slightest bit importance compared with love. This same chap tried to buy Harley Street or thereabouts to push Fenella into my arms and me into hers. I despise all this ploy. I turned down his deed of gift to me. Then I saw that you needn't beware of the Greeks who come bearing gifts. At least I could come to you with substance. I'm not after your lovely kingdom, only to steal your heart.'

My shoulders were aching with the grip he had of them and I eased them a little and laughed and told him I wasn't running away. I was running to him.

'Have you not known how long *I've* loved *you*? I think they are all trying to match-make, the household. That was a very fine proposal. It would have been just O.K. if you asked 'Madam, will you walk and talk with me?' It goes to music too.'

I slid my arms up round his neck.

'Yes, yes, yes, yes, yes, yes,' I laughed, 'and that's out of Joyce's *Ulysses* and I didn't learn it at school.'

He kissed me at the side of my mouth, as gently as a moth-wing then more firmly and at last he held me tightly as if he would never stop.

I thought that the household was almost certainly listening outside the door shamelessly by this and Annie would have the guile to look in through the key-hole. It had all been too quiet to be surgery business.

He had locked the door I knew and I went over and opened it quickly . . . caught Annie's eye with my own in the act. It seemed that the whole family had come with Annie, but she was the prime mover and she had the grace to blush in her shame. She took me into her arms and asked me if it was bad trouble for the family or for 'Himself'. Maybe it was the first time I had heard her give Jon my Grandfather's title and I knew the honour she did him.

'It's the best news, Annie. I hope it is happy ever after. It was a magnificent proposal and I jumped at him. I've loved him since the first day I saw him or thereabouts. So now we have a wedding to fix. I'm so happy I could die with it.'

There was a great excitement of congratulations and wishes for happiness. We talked over lunch and then a visit came in and I drove in the Daimler with him and while I waited for him, I remembered that tomorrow was Sunday and I had a date to take the police dog for a walk in the afternoon. I knew that Jonathan must now be told about the secret and he would want to come with me . . . no chance of him letting me go alone even with Sherlock Holmes. Tonight after dinner, I would tell as much as Jon would have to know. The others left us hours alone in the old nursery. The Bo'sun had lit an ash fire in the grate. I had to include James John of course and the childhood days, explain how it had been about Lucy. Then there had been the deaths . . . my father's and my mother's . . . and the last Dr Lister. Of course he knew most about Mrs Black's alleged attack and rape. Well, he knew the chicken-pox boy, Jimmy Black. Now I told him the Coon-skin-cap kid's secret and how secret it was. I was quite right that Jon refused to let me try the dead oak tree alone with Sherlock Holmes. He would be pleased to take us both. It was no good. He just would never let me go without his protection. He had seen the area and it was unspeakable. The wire had been impossible to break through, but he happened to know the telegraph poles had been blown down across the wire. If we went carefully we should be able to explore to see if the lost boy was there.

'It's in walking distance or we can walk most of it,' I said, but he ruled that out, said it was rough but the Daimler would cover most of the way with chains on the tyres. The white Alsatian could have the jump seat.

We talked about his uncle making the deed of gift to him. It would make a great difference to life, but the grand thing was that we could be wed. The money would make life easier for every member of Church House, but he would have asked me to marry him without it. He could not live without me and having held me in his arms, he knew he would die without me.

He started to make gentle love to me and I knew we were made for each other. I walked through the moon and the stars, and planets like space ships began to zoom past now and again, and back in circles like cornflakes on T.V. advertising. We went downstairs before it was very late. I knew Annie would be wondering what was going on. There was so much for us to discuss as family. Tomorrow was Sunday. Really it was time to put up the banns, but it would look a little bit hurried, or so the Bo'sun said and got a sharp reproof from Louisa.

Last of all we went to Louisa's room and said goodnight to small Sam and I broke off from the retinue and kissed Jon and thought of all the nights that stretched away before us. Jon was reading the lessons in church, and it

217

was the same bitter day. He left his overcoat off in the pew and walked up the aisle to the lectern and I knew that this was the man I would soon marry. The lessons were well chosen. The first was the first book of Genesis. When it came to the second, I took a deep breath for it was chosen from the Song of Solomon.

> Rise up, my love, my fair one and
> come away.
> For, lo, the winter is past, the rain is
> over and gone;
> The flowers appear on the earth;
> The time of singing of birds is come,
> and the voice of
> the turtle is heard in our land.

I wondered if he could hear my heart beat as he came back to me. I stopped at the police houses on the way home to tell Hacker that we would be calling for Sherlock Holmes after we had finished dinner. The doctor had insisted that he himself come with us and there was nothing to worry about. The ice would be fine. I grinned at Hacker, for we were both fen-bred.

'Crack she bear.
Bend she break.
In she go and no mistake.'

They all knew the jingle in the fens. 'You'll be O.K. with the doctor. If you put the chains on the Daimler, you could drive by the way we went when we lifted the froze-in floater that day, then work back out into the wilderness.' So in the afternoon Jon put the white Alsatian in the jump seat and we set out on high adventure.

# 10

We started off along the drift I had taken when I went with the police to lift the gypsy-boy's iced-in punt. It was a grey day and the clouds were threatening more snow to come. The going was rough as soon as we quit the High Street. This lane was used mostly to get to the cut.

It was deserted today and the chains were holding us well. I said it was like riding a bike on tram lines and Jon laughed and we were laughing easily today. He had no complaints or so he assured me. He had thought that the sky was sunny and blue, till he noticed the clouds gathering, had wondered where the brightness came from.

'It's a wind that would 'thrap' you, Jon, a six-coat day or is it seven . . . time you were learning the dialect, now you're going to live round ours!'

The cut ran from Agnes Parva behind Church House and we had reached to the place where we lifted the punt that day, hauling it up the bank with Len Marshall's tractor. Constable Tanner had been the expert and the punt was still 'in mothballs' in

Len's barn. I thought of the geography of the village. We only had to turn about and go along the High Street to the Conservative Club Corner, turn right for Len Marshall's shop and further on the barn. If you thought of it, we were travelling in a circle. I had had some sort of a craft on the cut as a girl, maybe a canoe or a little square-sterned dinghy. The cut was protected with flood banks. There was a wash between the banks, where the cattle grazed. We skated on the floods in the hard weather. The washes were famous for the skating championships. You could go for miles. We had come to the place to turn off now for the cut had taken a bend to the left. It got wider and deeper and the wilderness began. At last it was deserted and the village said the 'haunt' actually walked in the mere. Maybe we all believed in the poor woman who was supposed to have drowned herself. Our way was hard going now and the snow had drifted deeply into ridges and little hills. The chains were failing to hold us. We struggled along for a mile or so and then we skidded into a solid deep area of snow, where we burred to a halt with a screaming of chains.

We had got a sighting of the great oak now and we found the spade and dug out a parking place . . . a place for when the time came to go home again. The walking was difficult now. I let Sherlock Holmes off the leash and he was delighted, raced away ahead of us and showed off so that we knew how a good dog could behave and come back the moment he was summoned. It was strange how quickly the mist came down and the way got more and more hard to negotiate. I had studded shoes, but they did not stop me from two nasty falls one after the other, when my feet flew from under me and I was flat on my back. The fog was really a fog in no time at all. There was something quite sinister about it. The mere had a kind of miasma rising about it and the house was fading from sight. The sky was darker. It had that sort of look as if the end of the world was coming. The white dog seemed dramatically white now and to make things worse, he raised his muzzle to the heavens and howled. I tried to forget the 'haunt' and the way they said that she stood at the edge of the mere with the water running from her clothes and hair . . . grey hair too. We were at the edge of the iced-up mere at last and this was about where she would be. The water dripped into my imagination and there was a slushy patch, where the telegraph poles had been tidied away. I put the chain on the dog and made much of him for he had started to shiver. He was happier when I put my face down and told him that we might go home soon. I remembered what Hacker said to him and thought he understood me.

'Find. Find. There's a good boy. The boy is here somewhere. Find him for us.'

Presently we went up to the higher level and the house emerged more clearly. I hoped that Sherlock Holmes did not start to howl again as we turned away from the direction of home. Annie was quite certain that when a dog howled it meant a death. We were a superstitious lot in Agnes. The sound made most of us a bit uneasy. Jon said superstition was a sign of ignorance and he knew for a fact that Hacker's little daughter played the piano. On a visit once, 'Hepzibar' Hacker, aged about five, had given him a performance on the pianoforte; she had played chopsticks and the white Alsatian had 'sung'. It was not a good performance for a police dog, not a good performance for a busy G.P. He maybe was not healing the sick but maybe he was. In Agnes, he had found ways of curing patients that he had never read in the text books. I knew he was making himself a good name in the practice with mothers and children. Maybe like Gramp, God rest him, he believed in the humanities. Of course, Sherlock Holmes knew what we were saying. He knew it was time we were getting round to the search. I had turned my thoughts to the old tree house. It had changed over the many years. I knew James John would have come with us, but there was no point in starting off antagonism. Besides it was all a fearful secret. We had buried it and we wanted it marked top secret. Bullen agreed and so it was.

'A secret is a secret is a secret. Nobody must know about this escapade and especially Master James John, though he can hold his tongue. The doctor was in love with Miss Lalage from the day he saw her. He won't stand much chat about childhood sweethearts. Don't start all that stuff about nursery days or he'll go home and leave you with 'the haunt'.'

We got on with the search, took the dog to sniff round the base of the tree and he was interested at once. I went round to the door and saw the old knocker still, wondered how we had left it behind. It was a thing Gramp had found for us. A cast-iron knocker in the shape of a beautiful hand. You lifted it and knocked and it had a hollow deep echoing sound, that would have suited Marley's ghost. I remembered every detail of it. It was a thing of beauty. It had a verse on it that I knew by heart, by John Donne.

# BATTER MY HEART,
## THREE-PERSONED GOD
### FOR YOU AS YET BUT KNOCK,
### BREATHE, SHINE AND
### SEEK TO MEND.

'Is there anybody at home?' I heard Jon call loudly, but there was no reply.

I lifted the knocker and let it fall and I hoped it might not be calling the dead. The dog was down on his side scratching at the earth like Bill Sikes' dog. He was excited now and on the trace of something right enough. He began to climb the tree, branch to branch. He investigated the old deserted owl's nest, but it was empty, and the little white owlets long gone. Next winter maybe the owls would build there again. Just for now, the dog came down the tree from one step branch to another and came and looked up at us. It was quite obvious that the boy was still inside. I shouted to him that we had seen Jimmy Black and he had told us to bring some provisions. We had stuff in the car for the gypsy boy but he must come down.

The tree house glowered at us like as if he was the giant in Jack. Its great branches stretched out in despair.

'Come down and speak to us. We have cold bacon and beans for you. I'll make you hot

225

chocolate too and we'll have some. Come down quickly. The dog likes you. Remember the way you whistled to him last time, when they lifted the boat. I know this house, Squirrel Nutkin. I lived here for three years. It was prima.'

Jon walked away deliberately, turned his back on his thoughts. I looked up at the owl's nest and thought there was a hide in it. If the boy had a look-out there, he was watching every move we made. No doubt he understood nothing of what we said. It came to my mind the day of Gramp's funeral and how the Sally Army band had drawn Nutkin out of the tall chestnut, the red scarf at his throat.

> The Lord's my Shepherd,
> I'll not want.
> He makes me down to lie
> In pastures green, He leadeth me
> The quiet waters by.
> He leadeth me, He leadeth me,
> The quiet waters by.

He was at the look-out now and again in a bright-red scarf. At last I saw him. I decided to run out across the mere and pretend I was going, to see if he could be enticed down. It was then I saw him reach his hand out after me and the clouds were so low that it seemed he was groping for something. His hand might have picked something out of the cloud layer and held it to his chest and again I heard the strangest whistle on heaven or in hell. It was the same thing I had heard the other day and Sherlock was shattered by it, fell on his belly, and grovelled on the ice at my feet. Then he backed and left me, raced across the ice, to the door of the tree house.

There was a dripping sound that was all wrong and maybe meant a thaw. Jon had heard the whistle and now the dog was back at the old door and tearing it but I was past saving now. Bend, I felt the ice bend under my feet and the next moment, 'in I went and no mistake'. The water flooded over me, engulfed . . . invested me. I knew in the last moments I was done for. The darkness took my sight and my mouth was flooded with stinking rotten water like sewer filth. It invaded my ears and my eyes and my throat. I struck out and knew I was deep in the mere. I was through the ice and the escape was gone. I held my breath but knew air hunger. My feet kicked and found nothing. Again and again I struggled with my arms . . . nothing . . . nothing nothing, only the miasma of death, closing my eyes to dark for ever. I knew the evil spirit that ruled this place, a drowned woman, keening for a lost baby. Somewhere near but above me was the gibbet, terror in its arm, pointing the way to death. So now I was going to drown. I had no way to recall the whistle of the boy, that had called the dog again. Yet I had heard it before. I had no hope that even now Squirrel Nutkin was directing the dog. Only a splashing of an otter maybe and a leash that trailed my face. I recognised the links of the chain and grabbed at it, held it for my life. Jon's hand grabbed the neck of my sweater and I was hoisted up in the lift a fireman is trained to do. The sewer like filth emptied itself behind him and the life rushed back into me. I took a deep breath and another and a third. I found myself sitting down on a log and my sweater whipped off and his stethoscope on my chest wall and my breath coming smoothly and the pain going. I thought of the way I had fallen at his feet that day.

'I always come down a ladder like that' ... or something like that in bravado. 'I went in for a swim, but the ice isn't holding.' I croaked and felt the corduroy was about me and warm with his warmth and the antiseptic doctor smell he had, tight around me and his scarf warm and wool about my throat. I wondered where James John had gone. The white dog was familiar. He rolled in a bank of snow and tried to get his whiteness back and then he shuddered and shook himself and showered us with wetness and the boy had an old khaki towel and was drying him, making much of him, the dog adoring him. Of course James John was gone. He was a boy no more and it had happened a long time ago. I had no need to worry how cross Annie would be when we got home. I remembered my dead father and the big black greatcoat of uniform. By some magic it was very old and Jon was wearing it instead of his own jacket. My father had been killed in the Atlantic convoys and maybe Annie had given the jacket to the gypsy boy out of her mercy. It was the sort of thing she might have done or maybe my grandfather. I was very woosy and could not get my ideas to come straight. Here was the tree house and the cast-iron knocker . . . the hand. John Donne. Batter my heart, three person'd God. Had Jordan Ison given it to us? Was it Jordan Ison's hand cast the words? We should never have abandoned it. I was lifted to be carried in Jon's arms. The tree house had shrunk small with the years. It was right for Snow White now and her seven dwarfs . . . never the comfortable cottage I remembered, with the spiral staircase swirling round the play-room. It had been kept spotlessly tidy all the years. The table was still there and the small chairs and the dresser with the willow pattern plates and the wooden-handled knives. Jon sat me down upon a mattress of blanket-covered straw. The oil stove warmed the whole place and a kettle that steamed. My soaked wet shoes and socks and pants disappeared and I was dry and warm. We were drinking hot sweet tea and Jon covered me with an old blue horse blanket that I knew well as being ex-Will Papworth, who was given to digging people out of the snow, if they were doctors on midwifery cases. Mrs Smith had had her son that snowy night . . . a son after all the daughters. Jonathan put the stethoscope on my chest again and told me to breathe deeply, told me I would do now.

He explained the plan he had made. We were going home. It had to be done discreetly. He would walk back in the circle, come up at Len Marshall's barn . . . bring back Len and his tractor and the closed-in trailer full of straw. Some time, the Daimler must be collected. We would rendezvous at the Admiral Inn . . . keep Annie out of the secret, for secret it must be. Bullen would square the affair of Mistress Quickly. The case would be put underground, pigeonholed, unsolved. When I got home, I must dress properly and behave as if nothing had happened. Louisa would be able to produce fresh clothes and distract Annie from knowing what was going on. She and the Bo'sun were a match for Annie. Bullen must be summoned to the Admiral Benbow. It was clear that maybe Annie might be sent off to evening service. Better still she might be sent over to Sister Pepper's for a late supper.

'You'll never be able to work it,' I said but he kissed me and said he would take the police dog with him and return him to his base, see to getting him to P.C. Hacker and Hepzibah. She might give him a treat by playing chopsticks on the piano for him, and Sherlock could sing, ease the tension.

'You saved my life,' I said. 'You and the dog and Squirrel Nutkin. What can I do to reward the boy?'

'Let him live on in his world,' Jon said. 'That's what your grandfather said and saw to it being done.'

It was all quite impossible. I thought it over as I waited in the tree house for the trailer to come for me and the night came down in thick fog. There was no fear there and I found Squirrel Nutkin was all I had known him to be. I planned so many things to do, but knew they would be no great necessities for him. He was not one for television, discos or youth centres. Maybe he had a power that ruled the whole fen. It was certain that its animals worshipped him. In the quiet of the night, I found it quite possible to communicate with him and no word spoken between us. Don't ask me how, but he was able to let me know he was sorry I had not married James John, but glad I was to marry Jon.

The tractor came and fetched me away and Jon had collected the food for him that we had left in the car. He said goodbye in his own way gently stroking the wrought-iron knocker, laying it back in its place soundlessly, going back up the spiral staircase to safety and happiness and security.

Of course, I knew Agnes Parva as well as any of them, but I never understood how its underground worked. I do not doubt that a few of them knew what happened, but it was a confidence. People understood that there was no harm in Mistress Quickly and that it had all been a mistake. It was just one of those evenings, when her man had had 'his belt off at her', because he had drink taken. It was just a fen village and maybe there were others like it. Boys stole knickers off the clothes lines an odd time and were well thrashed for it if the fathers caught them in the act. They thought it a joke with a hazard in it, but at last when they were older, the drudgery of lifting the sugar beet in the winter knocked the mischief out of them.

There were always toads in Agnes Parva in the gardens and in the village green pool and in the willow beds. They were never known as anything but *Wendy Nightingale's Toads*. Wendy herself came to be a matron 'Up Lunnon' after a few years and she never made the same mistake again.

There was universal relief when the gypsy boy reappeared one day on his own in the same old way with the jackdaw on his shoulder. As usual, he said nothing and nobody expected anything else.

Little Sam was growing fast and he trailed round after his father and maybe the Almighty put out His hand to work a little miracle. The Bo'sun got no worse, 'only a smidgeon better . . . ' and better and better.

There had been the snow and now came the floods. My wedding to Jonathan took everybody's mind off all the disasters there had been in the last years. Agnes Parva reverted to being its old self and there was peace again too.

Life went on with its ups and downs and I had a son and then another. Jon and I had maybe started a dynasty of doctors. It meant perhaps that the step at the surgery would still be worn by footsteps.

It is a marvellous place, Agnes Parva, and

there are people who could tell you things you would never believe, but then who would ever believe in a haunted mere, or in a dead oak tree which housed a magical manikin squirrel . . . and a sinister gibbet outlined in a misty fen?

## THE END

*Other titles in the*
*Ulverscroft Large Print Series:*

# BLOODTIDE

## Bill Knox

When the Fishery Protection cruiser MARLIN was ordered to the Port Ard area off the north-west Scottish coast, Chief Officer Webb Carrick soon discovered that an old shipmate of Captain Shannon had been killed in a strange accident before they arrived. A drowned frogman, a reticent Russian officer and a dare-devil young fisherman were only a few of the ingredients to come together as Carrick tried to discover the truth. The key to it all was as deadly as it was unexpected.

# WISE VIRGIN

## Manda Mcgrath

Sisters Jean and Ailsa Leslie live on a small farm in the Scottish Grampians. Andrew Esplin, the local blacksmith, keeps a brotherly eye on the girls, loving Ailsa, the younger sister, from afar. Ailsa is in love with Stewart Morrison, who is working in Greenock. Jean is engaged to Alan Drummond, who has gone to Australia, intending to send for her when his prospects are good. But Jean shocks everyone when she elopes with Dunton from the big house . . .

# BEYOND THE NURSERY WINDOW

## Ruth Plant

Ruth Plant tells of her youth in a country vicarage in Staffordshire early in this century, a story she began in her earlier book NANNY AND I. Together with the occasional dip back into childhood memories of a nursery kingdom where Nanny reigned supreme, she ventures forth into a world of schooldays and visits to relatives, the exciting world of London and the theatre, the wonders of Bath and the beauties of the Lake District. She travels to Oberammergau, and sees Hitler on a visit there. On the threshold of life the future seems bright and war far away.

# THE FROZEN CEILING

## Rona Randall

When Tessa Pickard found the note amongst her father's possessions, instinct told her that THIS had been responsible for his suicide, not the professional disgrace which had ruined his career as a mountaineer and instructor. The note was cryptic, anonymous, and bore a Norwegian postmark. Tessa promptly set out for Norway, determined to trace the anonymous letter-writer, but unprepared for the drama she was to uncover — or that compelling Max Hyerdal, whom she met on board a Norwegian ship, was to change her whole life.

# GHOSTMAN

## Kenneth Royce

Jones boasted that he never forgot a face. When he was found dead outside the National Gallery it was assumed he had remembered one too many. The man he had claimed to have identified had been publicly executed in Moscow some years before. The presumed look-alike was called Mirek and his background stood up. The Security Service calls in Willie 'Glasshouse' Jackson — Jacko — as they realise that there is a more sinister aspect. Jacko and his assistant begin to unearth commercial and political corruption in which life is cheap and profits vast, as the killing machines swing into action.